Penguin Books
Appleby's Answer

Michael Innes is the pseudonym of J. I. M. Stewart, who was a Student of Christ Church, Oxford, from 1949 until his retirement in 1973. He was born in 1906 and was educated at Edinburgh Academy and Oriel College, Oxford. He was lecturer in English at the University of Leeds from 1930 to 1935, and spent the succeeding ten years as Jury Professor of English in the University of Adelaide, South Australia.

He has published several novels and two volumes of short stories under his own name, as well as many detective stories and broadcast scripts under the pseudonym of Michael Innes. His *Eight Modern Writers* appeared in 1963 as the final volume of *The Oxford History of English Literature*. Michael Innes is married and has five children.

Michael Innes

Appleby's Answer

Penguin Books

Penguin Books Ltd, Harmondsworth, Middlesex, England
Viking Penguin Inc., 40 West 23rd Street, New York, New York 10010, U.S.A.
Penguin Books Australia Ltd, Ringwood, Victoria, Australia
Penguin Books Canada Ltd, 2801 John Street, Markham, Ontario, Canada L3R 1B4
Penguin Books (N.Z.) Ltd, 182–190 Wairau Road, Auckland 10, New Zealand

First published by Victor Gollancz 1973
Published in Penguin Books 1978
Reprinted 1985

Printed and bound in Great Britain by
Cox & Wyman Ltd, Reading
Set in Monotype Times

Contents

Part One

British Rail

Chapter One

It was with gratifying frequency, nowadays, that Miss Pringle found herself sharing a railway compartment with some total stranger who was reading one of her books. And this was not all. During the last few years (since, to be precise, she had found an American as well as a British publisher) Miss Pringle had been in a position to treat herself to first-class tickets. It was her distinct impression that the upper stratum of society to which this indulgence had introduced her had more of a nose for, or in, her novels than had, when previously observed, the common herd who travel 'second'. (Miss Pringle, being almost elderly and instinctively old-fashioned as well, in fact referred to 'second' as 'third'.)

'Firsts', it was true, seemed as indisposed as 'thirds' to apply themselves to hardcover editions of Miss Pringle's increasingly celebrated books. With only the rarest exceptions, they were paperback readers, to a woman or a man. Miss Pringle at times found herself a little resenting this. It was surely a legitimate expectation that carriage-folk – and what are first-class passengers but the modern equivalent of these? – should be thinking, when they bought books, in terms of permanent and worthy accession to the substantial private libraries which doubtless dignified their homes. Consider, for instance, a baronet's library. (Miss Pringle's fictions often had one of these as crucial setting.) What could be more inappropriate to so august a chamber than a line of tattered old Penguins? And there was the question, too, of the rate of expenditure in a literary field consonant with, or seemly in relation to, other forms of expenditure. These people were certainly not paying, on average, less than a couple of guineas for their well-cushioned ride. Would not *one* guinea, and not what was now called twenty new pence, be a reasonable outlay upon the reading that would last them to the end of it?

But when these thoughts visited the journeying Miss Pringle

it is not to be supposed that it was to an effect of any marked acerbity of mind. Miss Pringle had achieved her modest eminence only after struggle. She had never, like Lord Byron, awakened one morning to find herself famous; she had in fact quite frequently awakened to morning papers which dismissed her latest brain-child in a couple of lines. It was only when *Vengeance at the Vicarage* had so providentially tumbled itself from the ample garments of the Archbishop of Canterbury as he stepped from an aeroplane, and she had thereupon worked night and day to finish *Revenge at the Rectory* six weeks later, that fortune had a little begun to smile upon her.

So what Miss Pringle chiefly felt now was simply that it was nice to be fairly widely read on any terms. Of course it would be even nicer if one day she contrived to hit the jackpot (as the young people mysteriously expressed it). At this very moment she had a sneaking feeling that *Poison at the Parsonage* (more than half-finished, and safely in the suitcase above her head) might do the trick. Meanwhile, it was agreeable to be favoured by the com-paratively few. Her publisher, a personable young man who had lately and quite charmingly taken to addressing her as his Dear Priscilla, teased her about being an *élitiste*. He appeared to have invented the word; it wasn't in her *Larousse*; but one got the idea. And the young man had been told by an uncle, the Dean of Barchester, that the Archbishop of York, first attracted by his senior colleague's inadvertent advertisement, had become a devoted follower of Inspector Catfish. Inspector Catfish was Miss Pringle's detective.

There appeared to be a high probability that the gentleman seated diagonally to herself in the compartment belonged to an *élite*, although perhaps one of birth rather than intellect. He was elderly; his droopy moustache held the particular tinge of brown which Sherlock Holmes would undoubtedly have known to pro-ceed only from the smoking of *Ramon Allones* (or would it be *Romeo y Julieta*?) cigars; and he was clothed in shapeless and shaggy tweeds. He looked, come to think of it, uncommonly like a baronet himself. And there he was – absorbed in *Murder in the Cathedral*. (*Her* work of that title; not the late Mr T. S. Eliot's.)

In paperback once more, it was true. But that, after all, intro-duced into the situation an element that Miss Pringle never ceased to experience as piquant and even in some degree alarming. The jackets of her hardcover books relied upon a bold typography for their effect. But the paperbacks led off with a stimulating, although entirely decorous, pictorial allurement on the front, and finished with a photograph of herself (herself and Orlando her cat) on the back. A spectacular recognition-scene was a possibility at any moment.

And now the gentleman, who was perhaps about to light a cigar, put down *Murder in the Cathedral*, open and covers upward, on the seat beside him. He produced – with a slight effect of anti-climax – a pipe and a tobacco-pouch. They were in a smoking-compartment. Nevertheless the gentleman looked straight at Miss Pringle and spoke.

'Madam,' he asked with grave courtesy, 'will you allow me?'

Miss Pringle fluttered into acquiescence. The fact that she had rather a line in gentlemanlike villains – particularly curates who had been to Eton and Cambridge and who appeared to be head-ing for a blameless berth among the Superior Clergy – sometimes inclined her to an irrational sense of guilt in the presence of gentle-men who (like her own late father the Archdeacon) *were* gentlemen in every sense. And the elderly man now lighting his pipe was certainly that. It wasn't merely that he talked (as her nephew Timothy would say in his slangy way) pucka posh and not synthetic posh. There was something about his bearing – or perhaps one might say his air – which told you at once that here was somebody flawlessly well-bred. *That air of aloofness and perfect diffidence which marks an English gentleman.* Miss Pringle was surprised at being unable to remember where she had read that. It had im-pressed her very much. She wasn't entirely sure that she hadn't, somewhere or other, quietly made use of it. Her long years of imaginative commerce with high life and criminal practice had necessarily a little impaired her moral character. But only a *very* little. Even when writing a book in an awful hurry, for example, she would never have purloined a whole paragraph. And a mere phrase or even a sentence, after all, might occur to anyone.

Miss Pringle's travelling-companion (and fan) had returned to his book. He was observably quite near the end of it. Perhaps he had got to the page on which the revolver was found behind the reredos, or even to the climactic moment of Inspector Catfish's discovering the missing cathedral plate in Canon Pantin's pantry. Unfortunately he didn't look terribly pleased. Indeed, behind the ogee-curve of his moustache his aristocratic features – for they *were* aristocratic – had settled into a mould of what could only be called sombre discouragement. Miss Pringle was distressed. She felt an impulse – for she was a proud and sensitive woman – to reach into her handbag, fish out twenty more or less new pence, and tender this reimbursement to her dissatisfied customer. But now she noticed that he was himself obeying some kindred fumbling manoeuvre.

He had produced a pencil. It was a distinguished pencil. It was in form a flattened oval; it was no more than an inch long; its value would have to be placed at something under a farthing (old style). But it lived with its tail in a little gold holder and its head in a little gold cap. It somehow didn't look the sort of writing-instrument for which one could obtain a refill; when the stubby little affair had been sharpened and whittled away you simply had to repair to some jeweller's shop in Bond Street and start all over again.

Miss Pringle (because she had an instinct for the minutiae of refined living) would have been much impressed by the mere appearance of this object had she not been so instantly depressed by the use to which she now saw it put. The stranger turned over the last few pages of *Murder in the Cathedral* – without even skimming them! – and inscribed beneath the final paragraph a sign which (since he then obligingly dropped the book on his knees) Miss Pringle was at once able to read. It was this:

$$'\beta - ? -$$

Miss Pringle not only read; she understood, since conversation with her erstwhile undergraduate nephew Timothy had taught her the elements of this dismal academic language. *Beta-minus-query-minus* was what you got from your tutor for a composition which somebody using plain English would call 'mediocre' or 'dull' or even perhaps 'dim'.

It might have been expected that a just indignation at so ungenerous a verdict would alone have occupied Miss Pringle's consciousness at this discomfiting moment. Actually, she was aware of other feelings as well. One was disappointment. The elderly man in the corner could not, after all, be a baronet. Baronets don't deal in betas, or in alphas and gammas either. It seemed more likely that he was a university professor. Miss Pringle had been brought up to hold the learned classes in high regard, but she was aware that these classes – indeed the liberal professions generally – were not quite what they had been in her father's time. Even the fellows of an Oxford college, she had been reliably told, might now be rather a mixed lot. Still, however that might be, there could be no doubt about this particular individual's social *ambiance*. And it was even possible – it suddenly came to her – that he was both a baronet and a professor as well. In the church there were certainly persons who held hereditary titles as well as being the Rector of this or the Lord Bishop of that. No doubt in the universities the same sort of thing occasionally occurred.

These thoughts (in an area in which Miss Pringle was prone to be rather foolish) were jostled by others (in an area in which she could occasionally be more perceptive than her unassuming profession required). As well as being injured by her travelling-companion's low rating of *Murder in the Cathedral* and disappointed by what she now had to judge ambiguous in his social situation she was intrigued by something elusive – that was the word – in the nature of his concluding reaction to her book. Deep in the constitution of the detective-story there is a large liability to end flatly or badly, and readers who have perused some 200 pages with satisfaction are often enough disproportionately censorious as they make their way through the score or so of pages with which it concludes. It is as if the ungrateful creatures were suddenly persuaded that they have been chewing straw. They may even be annoyed that this innutritious diet has been purveyed to them at an approximate rate of ten of those new pennies to the hour.

But this didn't seem to be quite what the gentleman with the ogee moustache was feeling. He wasn't registering irritation; he was registering gloom. And it came to Miss Pringle instinctively that her novel hadn't been judged and written off quite in terms of the simple canons of its craft. It was not with a literary critic that she was encapsulated in this snug and slightly overheated compartment. And this inclined Miss Pringle to a charitable view of her companion and his behaviour. For instance, she dismissed at once the thought that the recognition-scene had taken place; that the injurious scribble had been perpetrated, and cunningly offered to her regard, by one who had spotted her identity. He was a gentleman. He wouldn't do just that.

And now the situation developed. The elderly man began to evince certain small signs of physical discomfort characteristic of elderly men during the later stages of a railway journey. He shifted slightly in his seat. He discernibly estimated his distance from the door giving on to the corridor. He equally discernibly studied Miss Pringle's knees and feet – not lasciviously, but from a courteous impulse as little as possible to incommode a fellow-traveller. And then he knocked out his pipe, rose a shade stiffly to his feet, produced the ghost of a polite murmur, reached for the door beside her, and in a moment had vanished in quest of whatever convenience it had become incumbent upon him to seek. Miss Pringle was left alone – or alone except for the company of a harmless detective romance the quality of which had been most cruelly aspersed with the aid of an elegant gold pencil.

Miss Pringle's glance travelled, by an involuntary movement, to the suitcase perched on the rack in the further corner of the compartment. It revealed a luggage-label of that old-fashioned sort consisting of a leather sheath with a small celluloid window through which a visiting-card may be exhibited. It could be seen that such a card was actually on view, and it would be quite easy to stand up and examine it. Miss Pringle, who would have hated to be caught out in any unladylike act, hesitated. What if the owner of the suitcase had discovered what he sought to be 'engaged', and had decided that, rather than linger awkwardly in the corridor, he would simply return in temporary bafflement to his compartment? But Miss Pringle was a courageous woman, and she decided to risk it. What this resolution brought her was the following:

A. G. de P. Bulkington

Imperial Forces Club
Pall Mall, S.W.1

This was informative; yet, somehow, it was not quite informative enough. Miss Pringle's curiosity was but sharpened, and it was when thus vulnerably keyed-up that her attention was caught by something else. The gentleman's overcoat had been thrown carelessly on a vacant seat, with its lining – and in that lining an inner pocket – revealed. And peeping out from the pocket . . .

A strong tremor passed through Miss Pringle's frame. She felt like one standing on the brink of an awful chasm. What she saw was a letter, without a doubt. And a letter might tell much, or all!

Ladies do not trespass upon the private correspondence of gentlemen. On this there could be no conceivable argument. But are not lady-novelists a little different from *mere* ladies? Do they not possess a certain licence – even, in a sense, a certain duty – in the matter of possessing themselves as they can of whatever may the better inform them of the mysterious lives of the opposite sex? And all that seemed required, initially at least, was a mere tweak. The letter might simply have tumbled from the pocket! Miss Pringle tweaked, and found herself looking at an envelope thus directed in a sprawling hand:

Captain A. G. de P. Bulkington
'Kandahar'
Long Canings
Wilts.

At this moment Miss Pringle heard the sliding-door of the compartment open again. She relapsed abruptly into her seat – or rather into the seat opposite Captain Bulkington's. It was a very awkward moment.

Chapter Two

But Captain Bulkington seemed to notice nothing amiss. Perhaps he merely supposed that Miss Pringle preferred the view from this side of the train or imagined that she was avoiding a draught. He moved his overcoat a little, absently shoving the letter back into his pocket as he did so. He sat down, stiffly and this time with an audible creak, and slanted his legs unobtrusively in the manner necessary even in first-class carriages if one is to avoid an accidental flick or kick at opposing toes or ankles. All was well; nothing was going to be said. Miss Pringle, in consequence, was about to breathe freely (in a literal, not metaphorical sense, since she was a nervous woman) when she suddenly became aware of a fresh occasion of embarrassment. *Murder in the Cathedral* was lying on the floor of the compartment, with Orlando and herself uppermost. In her perturbed withdrawal she must have made some movement which had brushed it from the seat.

'Oh, dear – your book!' she exclaimed, and made a dive for it in a random and undignified fashion which might have suggested to anybody that she had mysteriously lost her head. And Captain Bulkington had, in fact, forestalled her. His own dive, if not exactly agile, had been more exact, and now the volume was in his hand. He glanced at the photograph, and he glanced at Miss Pringle.

'And *your* book, too,' he said.

The recognition-scene had taken place.

Miss Pringle had enjoyed an almost similar experience two or three times before. Still, not quite similar – and it was precisely the element of dissimilarity that would have made 'enjoyed' something of a misnomer now. She was still shaken by her narrow escape from being discovered in what would have been a most humiliating situation. And there is obvious difficulty in extracting pleasure from being identified as the authoress of a beta-minus-query-minus book. It was a little spurt of indignation that must have prompted the remark she now (with some surprise) heard herself offer.

'You didn't much like my novel,' she said. 'But I hope that you do at least like my cat.'

Captain Bulkington was startled – which was natural enough. He even glanced around the compartment and under its seats, as if supposing the lady to have referred to some actual feline co-partner in their colloquy. He also looked alarmed. Perhaps he owned a pathological fear of cats, and would have found Orlando in the flesh (or fur) not merely a brute *tertium quid* but positively what the witty Italians call a *terzo incomodo*. Then he became aware of Miss Pringle's politely pointing finger.

'Oh, I see!' he said. 'A delightful-looking creature, madam, 'pon my soul. But not got him with you – eh? In a basket, or anything of that kind?'

'When I have to travel, Orlando goes to a cats' hotel. A really good hotel, accepting only pedigree cats.' Miss Pringle provided this information quite cordially. The truth is that Captain Bulkington's ' 'pon my soul' had not a little enchanted her. She had never before actually met an English gentleman given to this antique locution, although she had come across it in novels, and even employed it in fiction herself, dowering with it some socially apposite character – a peer, perhaps, or what her father had used to call a Harrovian of the old school.

'Quite right,' Captain Bulkington was saying approvingly. 'One can't be too careful in choosing a well-bred cat's company, eh? Evil communications corrupt good manners. And Manners maketh Cat. True of Dog, too. Ha-ha!'

Miss Pringle joined in this conventional evocation of merriment. She had forgotten for the moment the Captain's invidious and dyslogistic employment of the Greek alphabet. She had been absolutely right in judging him (like Orlando) eminently well-bred. And now he further vindicated his possession of this character by boldly declining to flinch from the point of discomfort between them.

'That scribble, eh? Unfortunate misconception, madam. Word of honour. Bad habit of mine. Something I have to remember comes into my head, and I stick it down on whatever's in front of me. This time, it was a mark I'm simply bound in conscience to put into a pupil's report. His father won't relish it, I fear. But one's obliged to tell the truth.'

17

'A pupil? You are – ' Miss Pringle hesitated. She judged it awkward to say 'a schoolmaster'. Schoolmasters nowadays are liable to be people who go on strike, and thus definitely align themselves with the lower orders. 'A college tutor?' she ventured.

'A coach, madam. An old-fashioned crammer. Lads going into the Services mostly. Usually the Brigade.'

'Yes, of course.' This ready confirmation was rashly offered, since it turned upon Captain Bulkington's own possession of martial status, which was something she was not supposed to know about.

'Enjoyed your yarn very much,' the Captain said easily. 'Deuced ingenious. Dashed if I know how you people think of these things. Ladies particularly.'

'Women, as it happens, have been outstandingly successful at writing detective stories.'

'Perfectly true, perfectly true. Noticed it myself, 'pon my word.'

'It is what first directed my own attention to that branch of literature.'

'Jolly good. Dashed fortunate, if I may say so. World deprived of a lot of pleasure – innocent pleasure, eh? – if you'd taken up tragedies, or anything morbid of that sort.'

'I have always liked to think so.' Miss Pringle had flushed with satisfaction, for this was a genuine persuasion of her own. 'There are times when an absorbing yarn – you have used entirely the right word – provides distraction and solace, does it not? Times of anxiety, periods of illness or convalescence, even occasions of bereavement.'

'Bereavement?' Captain Bulkington looked doubtful. 'I'm not sure about that. Too much sudden death in your sort of thing, if you ask me, to be just right for reading after a funeral. Better than poetry, of course. When my poor father died – he had been in the regiment before me – the padre said he was sending me something called *In Memoriam*. Thought it would be one of those little notices you pay for in a newspaper. Turned out to be an interminable thing by Tennyson. Ring out wild bells, and so-forth. Queer stuff.'

'But extremely melodious,' Miss Pringle demurred. She didn't know quite what to make of this summary judgement. The Captain, presumably, employed an assistant to instruct his charges in

English literature. 'May I ask if you are a regular reader of detective fiction?'

'Regular?' Rather oddly, the Captain gave an impression of shying away from this. 'Pick one up on a bookstall from time to time. Or from our local library. Couple of shelves of them there. Grubby, rather. But dashed impracticable, most of them.' Captain Bulkington suddenly relapsed into his former gloom. 'I suppose *you* have to read the lot,' he said, rousing himself. 'Make sure somebody hasn't had the idea before.'

'Well, that can be an anxiety. Of course, one talks to one's fellow practitioners – to one's *confrères*.'

'And one's *consoeurs* too, eh? Ha-ha!' This learned witticism, although it struck Miss Pringle as displeasing, appeared to amuse Captain Bulkington very much.

'Something of the kind is the object of my present journey.' It was an occasion of gratification to Miss Pringle that she now had a secure footing among men (and women) of letters. She never failed to attend cocktail parties at the invitation of publishers; she went to lectures of a superior sort, followed by tea and discussion, such as are organized by the National Book League and the Society of Authors; she had even been given dinner by a distinguished fan in a rearward region of the Athenaeum. 'I have recently been elected to membership of the Crooks' Colloquium. Tonight is the occasion of our annual dinner. We call it the *Diner Dupin*. A little joke.'

'Crooks' Colloquium?' the Captain repeated blankly. 'Dupin?'

'Perhaps it ought really to be Tecs' Colloquium – only the alliteration wouldn't be so good. And Dupin, of course, is in honour of the great Poe.'

'The great po?' This, from a lady, appeared to leave the Captain a little shocked. 'In mess games our subalterns used to – But never mind.'

'Edgar Allan Poe, the founder of detective literature. At the annual dinner we are addressed by a guest of honour – usually an eminent criminologist. Tonight it is to be Sir John Appleby. I believe he was at one time head of the C.I.D. at New Scotland Yard. Or perhaps it was something even more distinguished than that.'

'Talking about cunning ways of bringing it off, eh?' New

horizons seemed to be opening before Captain Bulkington. 'Straight from the horse's mouth, and all that? Dashed interesting.'

'I don't at all know what subject he will choose. But he is said to have solved the most impenetrable mysteries. Real-life ones, that is.'

'Ah, real life!' The Captain had recaptured his sombre tone. 'The trouble with *you* people' – and he tapped Miss Pringle's book – 'is that you need such deuced peculiar circumstances. In this one, for example, you need a cathedral. Now, how is a fellow to come by that? A local parish church would be a different matter. But how, I repeat, is a fellow to come by a cathedral? It just isn't on.'

'I'm not sure that I quite follow you.' Miss Pringle was wondering whether, had she chosen a more modest ecclesiastical edifice as setting for the mystery in question, she would have rated a good beta-plus. She was also wondering, if only fleetingly, whether Captain Bulkington mightn't be a trifle mad.

'A mere random thought.' The Captain waved a dismissive hand. 'This crooks' affair – what else does it go in for?'

'We have a little quarterly journal, with articles on things that interest us – professionally, that is.'

'Good Lord! False beards, and silencers, and secret codes, and poisons unknown to science – all that?'

'Certainly things of that sort. And police procedure, and how criminal trials are really conducted, and so on. It is so important to get one's facts right. To control one's all too powerful imagination.'

'Can anybody buy the thing? Could I get it at Smith's?'

'Our journal? Well, no. One doesn't want such information in the wrong hands. Not in the hands of people making a living out of crime. One has to belong.'

'To this crooks' club? Can anybody join – I mean by paying a subscription?'

'Oh, no.' Miss Pringle tried not to betray amusement. 'One must have contributed to detective literature.'

'Published a yarn, eh? It can't be too hard to do that.'

'I suppose not.' Secretly, Miss Pringle did not agree. 'It's quite competitive,' she said.

'One would have to have a head for it, of course.' For some

moments Captain Bulkington brooded darkly. 'Thought of it myself, as a matter of fact.'

'A good many people have.'

'Rather jolly to have one's name to a book. Once started on a manual of cavalry training. Only, just then, they pretty well stopped having cavalry.'

'We shan't stop having crime.'

'Always with us, eh? You have a point there.'

During the course of this stimulating conversation the train had traversed the greater part of one of the home counties, and both Windsor Castle and Eton College Chapel (always agreeable objects in Miss Pringle's regard) had appeared briefly on the horizon. They were a signal, moreover, to begin preparing for the end of her journey, and she thought with satisfaction of the porters who, although now so diminished a band at the London railway termini, still had the trick of being available outside the first-class carriages. She would take a taxi to her well-appointed ladies' club (another fairly recent index of status and prosperity, this), where she would find her friend and fellow-writer, Barbara Vanderpump. Miss Vanderpump was the authoress of historical novels, but had been admitted to the Colloquium on the strength of dealings with certain deeply mysterious events associated with the career of Cardinal Richelieu. So they would go together to the *Diner Dupin*, having first severally applied themselves with proper concentration to the *grandes toilettes* they had elected for the occasion. It was probable that they would even have a glass of sherry before setting out, thus ensuring that they should be one up and at their liveliest in the event of any such crisis as having, for example, Sir John Appleby presented to them early in the proceedings.

All this was putting Miss Pringle in good humour, for she was a nice woman, finding contentment in simple things. She was even inclined to find contentment in Captain Bulkington of 'Kandahar', Long Canings, Wilts – although whether *he* was a simple thing was not exactly clear to her.

'Some devilish-queer experiences in India,' Captain Bulkington was saying. 'In the old days, that is. Might work up into something. As a thriller, I mean. Anybody ever offer you ideas – likely plots, and so on?'

21

'Oh, quite frequently. A great many people – and sometimes most surprising people – believe they know how to commit an undetectable murder. The trouble is, they quite often *are* undetectable.'

'But isn't that what you want?'

'Of course not. Think of poor Catfish.'

'Catfish?'

'The Detective-Inspector you've been reading about in my story. He has to *solve* his crimes, hasn't he? So they just mustn't be undetectable. It would never do. That's the point that Timothy misses.'

'Timothy Catfish?'

'No, no. Timothy is my nephew, and he has some very clever young scientists among his friends. They often bring me ideas that are no good at all. Either one would have to offer such obvious clues that the murder would be completely boring, or there could be no means of getting at it whatever. You see?'

'I believe I do.' Captain Bulkington was now (as novelists say) all attention; in fact he had bent on Miss Pringle a fascinated stare. 'Where does this Timothy live?'

'Timothy lives in London.'

'I mean, what is his address?' The Captain had actually produced a pocket-diary. 'I'd like to look him up.'

Miss Pringle now saw that her momentary, and seemingly bizarre, suspicion had been correct. Captain Bulkington was mad. She was so convinced of this that she glanced up nervously at the communication-cord. A notice beside it informed her that the penalty for its improper use had been raised from £5 to £20. But there are occasions upon which one has to face up boldly to the soaring cost of living. Miss Pringle felt she ought to risk it, and pull. Her story would be an improbable one, but at least she would have gained the protection of the guard. She half-rose, and then sank back in her seat.

'Timothy,' she heard herself saying firmly, 'is at present abroad.'

'A pity. He sounds a nice lad.' Quite amiably, Captain Bulkington had put the pocket-diary away again. 'May I ask whether you have ever collaborated with another writer?'

'I never have.'

'It might be quite an idea, wouldn't you say? Labour-saving, and so on. One partner provides the ideas, and the other sweats it out on the typewriter.'

'I am sure that I should not myself take satisfaction in such a division of labour.'

'Or perhaps one do the whole job, and the other simply provide the working capital.'

'The working capital?'

'Well – ha-ha!' – while the grass grows the steed mustn't starve. Say five hundred down, and both names on the title-page. How about it?'

'You appear to be proposing a peculiar variant of what is called vanity publishing.' Miss Pringle had decided that, after all, Captain Bulkington was harmless. 'A sort of ghost-writing.'

'Call it what you like. But it would get a fellow in with that Colloquium crowd – journal and all?'

As he asked this, the Captain got to his feet, and made a sudden lurch towards Miss Pringle. Her alarm was renewed, and then the thought suddenly occurred to her that she had perhaps been travelling with a drunkard. But Captain Bulkington didn't smell of drink. And at once she realized that he had simply risen to secure his suitcase, and that his loss of balance had been occasioned merely by the train's passing over some complicated system of points as it approached Paddington.

'Venture to give you my card,' the Captain said. 'Hope you won't consider it impertinent. Professional matter, eh? We might fix something up between us yet. Basis, as they say, of mutual advantage. Shall remain great admirer of yours, in any case.'

Miss Pringle had, of course, no need of Captain Bulkington's card. His address was engraved on her memory as securely as on any piece of pasteboard, and she could find him if she wanted to – although no contingency could be less probable. But he hadn't, so far, so much as mentioned his own name, and it would be rather rude simply to reject this valedictory gesture. She wouldn't, naturally, give him *her* address, nor would her publisher divulge it to him without permission. So there was no great risk of this eccentric character's proving a nuisance. Perhaps if she accepted the card with a faintly indicated air of amused indulgence he would take a hint from that. Miss Pringle evinced such an air, or hoped she did, and put the card in her bag.

'How very charming of you,' she said in an appropriately conventional tone. 'I shall remember our interesting talk. And now I must say good-bye.'

The train had, in fact, come to a halt, and Captain Bulkington was gallantly getting her suitcase down from the rack and pulling back the door of the compartment. Although so curiously deranged, there was no question of his agreeable manners. No doubt he had himself been in what he called the Brigade – which meant the soldiers who looked so splendid when the Colours were trooped, or the Guard was changed at Buckingham Palace. He might even be personally known to the Queen, or at least to the Duke of Edinburgh. Miss Pringle decided to go so far as to shake hands.

'Share a taxi, perhaps?' the Captain suggested hopefully. 'Small economies necessary, these days. All those damned taxes.'

'Thank you, but I am being met by friends.' Miss Pringle rather prided herself upon her adroitness with small social lies; she even believed that she could manage quite a big lie at a pinch. 'In the station hotel,' she added, by way of obviating any awkwardness on the platform.

'Then *au revoir*,' Captain Bulkington said easily. 'Hope you have a jolly dinner. And pick up a tip or two, eh? I'll be on the lookout for your next.'

'That will be extremely nice of you.'

And thus Miss Pringle escaped into the almost open air of Paddington.

Chapter Three

'My dear Priscilla, you have made a conquest, I declare!' Miss Vanderpump spoke with what she would herself have described as a merry tinkle in her voice. She tapped the card her friend had shown her – so vivaciously that her sherry jumped in its glass. 'A beau – and a military officer!' Being what is called a romantic novelist, Barbara Vanderpump felt it incumbent upon her to employ a slightly antique vocabulary. 'And, you say, *un vert galant.*'

'Just what does that mean?'

'It means that you report his joints creaked.' Miss Vanderpump bubbled. 'Do you think he is a Hussar? Or a Dragoon?'

'He is certainly neither now. He appears to be a pedagogue.'

'Which lends rather a sinister resonance to his address.'

'Kandahar?' Miss Pringle was perplexed.

'No, no. Long Canings. He is a most prodigious fustigator of small boys.'

'Barbara, you are extremely foolish. A crammer takes on nineteen-year-old youths, who have been superannuated from the public schools. Boys who have been hopeless even in an Army Class. He prepares them for Sandhurst, and places of that sort. It must be a depressing means of livelihood.'

'My dear, we are out of date, don't you think? It seems probable that, in these egalitarian times, Sandhurst is no longer entered in that way. Your new friend no doubt coaches his charges for admission to strange new universities. Which is worse and worse. Captain Bulkington is a figure of pathos, I declare. Did he seem very hard up?'

'He offered me five hundred pounds.'

'Five hundred pounds!' Miss Vanderpump stared. 'To – ?'

'It appeared to be to collaborate on a detective novel.'

'Then he must, as you have conjectured, be a little unhinged. He probably hasn't a penny.'

'He belongs to a very good club. One of those in Pall Mall.'

'However do you know that? Did he propose an assignation there?'

'He well might have. But it was simply' – Miss Pringle was a little embarrassed – 'that I happened to notice a luggage-label on his suitcase.'

'And you belong to a very good club yourself.' Miss Vanderpump glanced appreciatively round the drawing-room of the Lysistrata. 'You must invite him to luncheon here. And invite me as well. I'd love to meet the *inamorato*.'

'I will do nothing of the sort.' Miss Pringle applied herself to her own sherry. She sometimes found Miss Vanderpump's resolute pursuit of spirited conversation a shade fatiguing. 'For that matter, he would much prefer to be asked to the Colloquium. He has this thing about crime-writing. I think he would call it crime-writing. An odious expression.'

'It sounds almost fishy.'

'Fishy?' A pause ensued, while Miss Pringle lit a cigarette. 'Nothing of the kind has occurred to me. He was, in his way, quite an amiable man.'

. 'You must not speak of him in a past tense. You and he have a future together. I feel it in my bones.'

'Then *your* bones creak, my dear woman. The episode was amusing while it lasted. But I was most careful to deny him any means of following it up.'

'That was unadventurous. Any why *not* collaborate with him? Of course, Priscilla, you are now so extremely successful that his suggestion of a fee is an absurdity. But you could make your own arrangement about dividing the royalties, after all.'

'You are talking very great nonsense, Barbara. What rational motive could prompt me to such a course?'

'It needn't be strictly rational. It might be a matter of your doing something kind.'

Miss Pringle was so surprised that she finished her sherry at a gulp. This was a mistake, since at least twenty minutes must elapse before the two talented ladies could usefully set out for the *Diner Dupin*. Moreover, she was now constrained to notice that Miss Vanderpump's was also an empty glass. Although far from grudging the cost of a further *apéritif*, she was conscious of liking, upon formal occasions, to keep a clear head. It was all very well for Barbara, whose line was the artistic temperament and a dashing vivacity. She herself preferred to give an impression of cool intelligence – which is the proper endowment, surely of writers of the classical detective novel. However, she believed she didn't get tipsy very easily. So she asked for more sherry.

'Of my doing something kind?' she asked.

'Certainly. This Captain Bulkington – surrounded by his horrible half-wit youths, and not even able to beat them – probably leads a very dull life. A lonely life, too. What he seeks is simply some pleasant professional association. And you would benefit from it yourself, Priscilla. As a writer, that is. Haven't some of the reviewers been saying that you have rather run the clergy to death? Literally to death, more often than not. Your art might well benefit from fresh associations. You could stay at "Kandahar" – '

'That would be most improper.'

'There is probably a respectable matron or housekeeper or the like who would preserve the *convenances*. And think of all those youths. They would make a fascinating study. Several of them would probably fall in love with you. Those from long-broken homes, for instance, who have never known a mother.'

'Or even a maiden aunt.' Miss Pringle spoke tartly. Barbara's delightful nonsense could be extremely tiresome. 'You seem to be much more obsessed with this man than I am. Why not pick him up, and collaborate with him yourself?'

'Why not, indeed?' Miss Vanderpump waved her replenished glass gaily. 'Collaborate, that is. The expression "pick him up" is a somewhat indelicate one. Or why should we not all three collaborate? It would be the greatest fun. Captain Bulkington no doubt takes a keen interest in military history. A romance of the Napoleonic Wars, perhaps. A title comes to me like a flash! *Revelry by Night.* The reference would be to the Duchess of Richmond's ball in Brussels on the eve of Waterloo. At the same time, it would be *un mot à double entente* –'

'Which, I suppose, is the correct French for what most of us call a *double entendre?*'

'Exactly. And we should be in rivalry with Thackeray in *Vanity Fair*, not to speak of Lord Byron in *Childe Harold*. Of course there would be a mystery element, Priscilla, such as only you could provide.'

'Thank you. But I don't think Captain Bulkington would be interested in historical romance, even with mysterious corpses thrown in. His taste is for the small-scale and the everyday. He was discontented with *Murder in the Cathedral* because the cathedral wasn't something more manageable, such as a parish church. How, he asked me, is a fellow to come by a cathedral?'

'My dear Priscilla, if that isn't fishy, what *could* be fishy? Captain Bulkington is a homicidal maniac.' Miss Vanderpump had recklessly changed ground. 'He lives amid fantasies of cunningly contrived murder. He dreams of possessing himself of diabolical infernal machines and poisons unknown to toxicology. When he discovered who you were, you inevitably went to his head.'

'And you regard all this as a good reason for collaborating with him?'

'Certainly. There is scope in Captain Bulkington for the most fascinating psychological study.'

'I think it would be better if his mind were diverted to the Battle of Waterloo.' Although speaking lightly, Miss Pringle was conscious of feeling considerable perturbation. She was far from certain that there was not some germ of truth in Barbara Vanderpump's frolicsome interpretation of her adventure. 'Do you think,' she asked impulsively, 'that I ought to tell the police?' She paused. 'Seriously, Barbara?'

'Perhaps you should. Why not tell this interesting man Appleby, whom we are going to meet tonight?'

'I don't think that would quite do. Hasn't he retired? And, in any case, it would not be suitable on a social occasion.'

'I am unable to agree – not, Priscilla dear, if you do it with proper address. Simply tell him, as if purely for amusement, of this rather odd encounter on your way up to town. And let him draw his own conclusions. Even if he no longer runs all the policemen, he might drop a word somewhere, so that discreet inquiries would be made. Yes – I believe it is really your duty to do just that. Otherwise, quite dreadful things may happen. *The Killings at Kandahar. Crime at a Crammer's. The Witness from Wilts.*' Miss Vanderpump produced what the poet Meredith would have called a volley of silvery laughter. 'My dear, you must forgive me,' she said. 'I am hopelessly in thrall to the Comic Spirit. There was a star danced, you know, and under that I was born.'

Miss Pringle gathered up her evening-cloak, and made no reply. She was telling herself that she had quite forgotten how really silly Barbara Vanderpump was. And of her afternoon's adventure she was sorry that she had told her a thing.

It was the first of London's evening rush-hours, and their taxi made only a tedious stop-go progress towards the Café Royal. Fortunately the Comic Spirit had suspended its overlordship of Miss Vanderpump – perhaps the better to put her through her paces in more brilliant company later on. Miss Pringle thus had leisure to look around her, and she was far from feeling impatient merely because their progress was rather slow. She had made her home of recent years in a retired situation (but where there was a good vicar) near Worcester, and a visit to London was really like a child's treat. It was only *that*, of course, because it was infrequent – and this made her glad that she had decided against living in the capital. A London home would require money – really a lot of money – and it was still only on her own modest scale that she could think of herself as affluent now. Of course, if one was famous, and not just established (although 'established' was a comfortable word, and not to be despised), it would be another matter . . .

They were in Shaftesbury Avenue, and it was like going through a 'scenic' railway in a Brobdingnagian fun-fair. The multicoloured neon signs flickered rapidly on and off, leaving the most bewildering after-images on the retina; other brilliant lights pursued each other helter-skelter in circles and squares and oblongs and elaborate arabesques. One of the theatres kept on flashing the name of some currently successful playwright very rapidly in green and red and blue – first in one colour and then another. Childishly, Miss Pringle shut her eyes and tried to see the same lights announcing PRISCILLA PRINGLE with equal abandon. Although she didn't achieve a very convincing image, the thought was an exciting one, all the same. It remained with her, intoxicatingly, as the taxi wove its way down Haymarket and up to Piccadilly Circus, and came to a halt.

'They don't advertise *us* like that!' she said a little breathlessly, as she jumped out.

'Us?'

'Novelists.'

'Advertisements don't sell novels.' Miss Vanderpump prided herself on understanding publishing. 'What does, nobody knows.'

'Advertisements like those might.' Miss Pringle gestured in the direction from which they had come, although she had to interrupt fumbling in her bag for coins in order to do so.

'It wouldn't pay, you dear goose.' Miss Vanderpump's laughter, at its most argentine, startled the large man in a top-hat who was holding open the door of the taxi. 'Perhaps we ought to turn playwrights. The idea of costume drama has always attracted me. But wouldn't you say that large success is a little vulgar?'

'One would at least wish to avoid notoriety,' Miss Pringle replied judiciously.

And the two ladies repaired to their banquet.

Chapter Four

Appleby at sixty had to keep on reminding himself that sixty it was. He no longer felt like Appleby at twenty, but it wasn't at all clear to him that he and Appleby at, say, thirty were not very much one and the same person. At least curiosity had not died in him; if it had, he would not have come to this dinner. Thomas Hardy has a poem in which the moon peers in upon Thomas Hardy scribbling at his desk – being interested in the 'blinkered mind' (as he brutally tells the poet) of somebody at all prompted thus to scribble 'in a world of such a kind'. Appleby felt rather like the moon – at least in relation to people who invent crimes in a world so deplorably full of crime already. He wanted to peer at them.

It wasn't perhaps, quite the spirit – he told himself – in which to have accepted an invitation to turn up as principal guest at a feast. But then, after all, if he was peering he was also being peered at His hosts (and hostesses), creators of the golden world of fiction, were not without their own curiosity about him as an emanation from the brazen world of fact. He had *actually* sat in an office overlooking the Thames, with high-powered Detective-Inspectors and the like presenting themselves to report on this and that; he had *actually* – only a little earlier in his career – hurried in an equally high-powered police car to inspect one more-or-less enigmatical corpse or another. And now he was at their dinner, decently able to say the right, the appreciative, thing to people he had never heard of, and presently proposing to get on his feet and make a speech which at least would offend nobody. One way and another, it was a reasonably fair deal.

Already, and before sitting down, he had made a bow to several presumably deeply crime-stained ladies, and had had introduced to him an answering number of gentlemen doubtless reeking (could one have but sniffed it) of gore. And of chloroform, of course, and of gunpowder or whatever now propels bullets from revolvers, and of that peculiar smell as of bitter almonds inseparable from any really high-class poisoning. Appleby had found all these people agreeable and quite fun; his only anxiety had been to deal with the fact – if it arose – that a preoccupied life had positively forbidden him the pleasure of ever reading anything they had written. But it hadn't arisen – or rather it had arisen instantly to evaporate, since they had all taken it for granted at the start that the sad fact must be precisely so. They were rather modest people, really – which was not a condition of mind which he had ever been much conscious of registering in such forays as he had ventured into more exalted literary spheres. Appleby resolved to excise from his speech one or two mild ironies which had been forming themselves in his head. There *were* a surprising number of women, for one thing. Appleby, who was old-fashioned (as old-fashioned, if the truth may be uttered, as that Miss Pringle whom we have lately met), believed that, *vis-à-vis* ladies, anything approximating to banter wasn't at all the thing.

He had looked round, on entering, on the offchance of a familiar face. And two familiar faces – for they arranged things very well – in fact flanked him at table now. He had known Miss Barrace for years – known her as a lady with a 'desk', as they said, at the Foreign Office. He just hadn't known that Miss Barrace was Miss Somebody Else as well, and decidedly at the top of that lethal tree in the numerous limbs of which he had, for the evening, been invited to scramble. Miss Barrace was tremendous. He wasn't confident that there didn't already show at least a light sweat upon his brow as a consequence of the intellectual effort required to give her anything like a conversational *quid pro quo* or tit for tat. With old Hussey on his other hand it was possible to be more relaxed, although old Hussey was at least equally eminent. He was Master of Appleby forgot just what Cambridge college, a power in the land at something called Greek Epigraphy, and given, every decade or so, to uttering some deep mystery in the tradition of Douglas and Margaret Cole or Ronnie Knox. Appleby *had* once read a novel by Hussey. It had been called *The Seventeenth Suspect*. And he did at least recall of it that the anterior sixteen had all been given a very fair spin.

The *Diner Dupin* was appropriately mounted. In the place of honour – hard by Miss Barrace, that is to say – reposed a tatty letter-rack, decidedly an authentic period piece, in the criss-cross tapes of which was thrust an equally tatty envelope. Opposite Miss Barrace, as the presiding genius of the feast, was a ferocious (but stuffed) orang-outang (or was it gorilla?) such as the severely logical mind of the great Dupin had once inferred as the only possible efficient cause of the regrettable events in the Rue Morgue. Appleby belonged to a dining club called the Peacocks, existing to honour the shade of Thomas Love of that name; he made a mental note to endeavour to borrow for one of its occasions a creature so eminently able to recall the prince of all such beasts, Sir Oran Haut-Ton. He ventured, indeed, to put this to Miss Barrace now, with the consequence that he was instantly subjected to a stiff *viva-voce* examination not only on *Melincourt* but on *Crochet Castle* and *Gryll Grange* as well. Quite soon he was telling himself that the grotesquely named Crooks' Colloquium was a wholly pleasurable affair.

'Going to clobber us, I suppose?' the venerable Hussey was saying.

'Clobber you? My dear fellow, nothing is further from my mind.' Appleby was all surprise. 'You get clobbered?'

'Lord, yes! It's absolutely the thing from our distinguished guests. Heavies from the criminal bar. Home Office experts on entrails and heaven knows what. Unfortunate chaps who look after homicidal maniacs in jug. They get up and tell us we touch pitch and shall not pass undefiled. They must be absolutely right.'

'It's not a line of thought that had ever come to me.'

'Don't be mendacious, Appleby. It doesn't become your years. At our last jollification of this sort we had a fellow from your own old stamping-ground at the C.I.D. A mild-mannered man. But he felt he must stand up and be counted. He simply appealed to us to give over. To chuck it. To purge and live clean. One day, he said, one of us might put something in somebody's head.'

'Did he claim that it had happened already?'

'I don't know that he did. Although forthright, he was a tactful and compassionate man. What do *you* think?'

'I'd suppose it more likely to work the other way. Your colleagues' – Appleby glanced round the table – 'occasionally collect a few tips from the world of real crime. But they then fantasticate them in a manner that takes them clean out of the realm of the possible. No criminal would waste time in putting himself to school amid such fairytales.'

'You relieve my mind greatly.' Hussey sounded, in fact, rather disappointed. 'My own first story was about a peculiarly ingenious murder in a Cambridge college. I knew nothing whatever about such places. I had been no more than an undergraduate in one. And undergraduates, of course, know nothing. Nothing at all.'

'About their seniors? I can imagine that to be so. Why should they? They have other matters to attend to.'

'Exactly. Well, I eventually returned to my own old college as a Fellow. It was a most urbane society. Or so I judged for a while. Then I observed that there were frictions here and there. Subacute irritations. Irritations which could not, in honesty, be so described. Unspeakable passions, my dear Appleby, and unquenchable animosities! I lived for months in terror lest one of these phrenetic scholars should chance upon my book, and that comprehensive holocaust should succeed.'

'But it didn't?'

'You are perfectly right. It didn't. And everything subsided, and we became a very clubbable crowd.'

'Just so. And if one of your temporarily incensed colleagues *had* come upon your romance, the idea of putting such implausible nonsense into practice would never have entered his agitated but highly intelligent head.'

'I call that a damned uncivil speech.' Hussey chuckled and raised his glass in amiable salute. 'But let there be enough agitation, you know, and intelligence fades out. What if one of these chaps had gone right off his chump?'

'I give you that.' Appleby raised his own glass. 'If he were mad enough, he might start conning a whole library of thrillers. But a man who is both sane and intelligent, and who wants to kill somebody and get away with it, is likely to think his little problem out for himself. He will probably see the advantage of being as dead simple as may be.'

'Dead's the word.' Miss Barrace, who had been listening, interrupted briskly. 'But, no doubt, there are people whose instinct it is to look for printed instructions. A good supply of arsenic fails to command their confidence unless the recommended dose is printed on the bottle. And Dr Hussey's Cambridge colleagues would have an inclination that way – viewing everything, as somebody said, through the spectacles of books. But I agree with Sir John. They wouldn't be likely to get much that was useful out of detective stories. They'd do better to engage in a little research in the annals of actual crime. Famous Trials, and that sort of thing.'

'Sordid,' Hussey said disapprovingly. 'All that stuff about pathologists coming forward and giving in evidence just what they found in the various sealed jars brought to their labs. Until it has been what Appleby calls fantasticated by you and me, Miss Barrace, violent crime is merely squalid and disgusting.'

'Perhaps so,' Miss Barrace said. 'But – do you know? – I once met a respectable elderly gentleman who was approaching things decidedly from the text-book angle. But not violent crime. Only blackmail. He did me the honour of consulting me on the subject.'

'He came to you,' Appleby asked, 'and confided to you that he was the victim of a blackmailer? I've been the recipient of such confidences myself in my time.'

'No, no – nothing of the kind. He didn't come to me, for one thing. It was a casual encounter on a railway journey.'

'How very odd.'

'And it was my impression not that he was being blackmailed, but that he was proposing to set up as a blackmailer. And he had, as it were, those printed instructions I was speaking of. He was reading the thing up.'

'Most interesting,' Hussey said. 'A scholar, no doubt.'

'Well, no. He said nothing about his walk in life. But I believe I should have concluded him to be an unsuccessful military man.'

'A military man?' Appleby echoed, looking up. 'And on a railway journey, you said?'

'Yes, indeed.' Miss Barrace did more than masculine justice to the brandy which had now arrived before her. 'And railway journeys are either restful or boring, as one feels disposed. I was bored, and quite welcomed this odd character.'

'And blackmail, you said – not murder?'

'I did say. You need not nod off, Sir John, after so trifling and foolish a banquet.'

'I beg your pardon.' Because he had the habit of noting everything, Appleby noted the totally irrelevant fact that Miss Barrace had quoted from *Romeo and Juliet*. 'And I assure you I am most interested. So is Hussey. Please go on.'

'He was plainly aggrieved by the book he was reading. It was some sort of legal textbook on blackmail. We entered into conversation. He asked me if it was a subject I was interested in. I had to confess having had more than one occasion to look into it.'

'But of course,' Hussey said cordially. 'It occurs in at least one of your tip-top stories. I remember them well.'

'Nothing of the kind, Master. Pray desist from idle flattery. My interest was a consequence of what impertinent reviewers are disposed to call my other character. Not that blackmail – except of the very most genteel and velvet-glove sort – much turns up in the routine work of the F.O. But during the war I had to branch out a little, and look into certain aspects of espionage.'

'You certainly had to do *that*,' Appleby said. Fabulous stories about Miss Barrace were coming back to him.

'Far more spies are created through blackmail than by the enticement of a comfortable numbered account in a Swiss bank. But that is commonplace to you, Sir John.'

'It is. A pretty ghastly sort of commonplace, often enough.'

'Of course. Fear, not greed, is the mainspring of that whole futile industry. But we digress.'

'So we do. And within ten minutes you will be calling upon me to get up and talk nonsense. So let us press on. Just why was this military character aggrieved by his textbook?'

'It seemed to be because it was all about blackmailers being caught out. Just how the law can be exercised to cover and successfully send down even the most cunning of them. It wasn't in the least what the colonel – I am imagining him to be a colonel – was after.'

'On the contrary,' Hussey prompted, 'he wanted tips on how to bring the thing off?'

'Precisely. But he wasn't an unintelligent old rascal. He was aware of the value – call it the negative value – of cautionary tales. But he wanted, so to speak, the positive know-how.'

'Which you would have been very well able to provide.' Hussey chuckled. 'But it wouldn't have been altogether moral to oblige him.'

'One has one's professional obligations.' Alarmingly, Miss Barrace responded to Hussey's chuckle with a deep and rumbling laugh. 'I could hardly offer him even the small change of the subject.'

'Was he mad?' Appleby asked.

'It must be evident that an element of eccentricity entered into his attitude.' Miss Barrace paused upon this eminently diplomatic reply. 'Waiter, more brandy.'

'And then?'

'He suggested that we might have further chats. It seemed not feasible, alas, that they should take place. So that is the end of my story. But I confess that I was left feeling curious about him.'

'A wholesome attitude,' Appleby said. 'Did you, by any chance, exchange names?'

'Certainly not. He did, in fact, offer me his card. I tore it up on the platform without looking at it. It was either that, or taking an absurd story to the police.'

'So it was.' Appleby was so impressed by this latest piece of information that quite a pause succeeded. 'By the way,' he said, 'I am interested in some of the members of your club. Those two women at the far end of the table, for instance – the one in salmon-pink and the other in magenta. Who are they?'

'I'm afraid I don't know their names. They are recent accessions to our number, and I fear I am not quite keeping up. I think the salmon-pink one writes stories about archdeacons and prebendaries and precentors. Why should those in particular – ?'

'They were introduced to me – or introduced themselves – in a confused sort of way. The magenta one was anxious that the salmon-pink one should tell me some interesting anecdote.' Appleby just perceptibly hesitated. 'There was to be a railway journey in it, and a retired soldier. But the salmon-pink one rather shut the other one up.'

'Then you were no doubt preserved from some entirely boring communication. During the informal aftermath of this' – Miss Barrace was grim – 'quite a number of people will want to tell you things. And now, Sir John, are you ready?'

'I believe I'd claim readiness as one of my few remaining virtues.'

'Good,' Miss Barrace said. And she tapped on the table and stood up.

Part Two

In Darkest Wilts

Chapter Five

Miss Priscilla Pringle to Miss Barbara Vanderpump

MY DEAR BARBARA,

No, I think I shall not be in town again for some time, but of course we must certainly lunch together when I do come up! I have finished *Poison at the Parsonage*, I am thankful to announce, if only after one or two bad moments. Needless to say, there was no trouble with the ecclesiastical part, because I know that territory thoroughly. But the whole episode of the unprincipled farmer who thought he was shooting a fox (although it was really the red-haired Lady Curricle, who had 'taken a toss', you will remember, over a hedge) was, I fear, a mistake. I have never myself ridden to hounds (although my Uncle Arthur was an enthusiast and celebrated as a most intrepid 'thruster' in his time), and found considerable difficulty in catching the feel of a fast run with the sagacious animals! But now I think it will at least pass. I found just a little help, I will confess to you, in Siegfried Sassoon's *Memoirs of a Fox-Hunting Man*.

Speaking of parsonages, do you recall my odd encounter with Captain Bulkington, about which you were so anxious that I should tell that important policeman, Appleby? Well, I recently met somebody from his, Bulkington's, part of the country (which is near Chippenham) and she told me that the proper name of 'Kandahar', the Captain's house, is simply The Old Rectory, Long Canings. The parish of Long Canings was combined a good many years ago with the neighbouring parish of Gibber Porcorum. At that time the Captain must have bought the house from the Ecclesiastical Commissioners and given it its present fancy name, which no doubt commemorates same family association of his own. And talking, by the way, of names, it appears that Long Canings is so called after an interesting rural pursuit, long practised there. I must find out more about this.

But I want to find out more about something else. The Old Rectory is not really old at all – and indeed parsons' houses thus denominated seldom are. In the mid-nineteenth century, when (as you will know) the beneficed clergy were still persons of position, and owning a stake in the country, it was the frequent habit to build vicarages and the like which often overshadowed, in point of respectability and consequence, the local public house (dear me, I mean of course to write manor house!) itself. Our quaint Captain's residence is said to be like this: an imposing Victorian pile in the Gothic taste. It was thus no doubt suitable for the reception of the extensive tutorial establishment he designed.

But why, you ask, am I interested in the place? Well it seems that the last incumbent actually to live there came to a violent and mysterious end! He was murdered! It is quite notable how seldom this happens to clergymen in real life, so an authentic instance is naturally of interest to me. And I have a notion that just a peep at the scene (although not, of course, exposing myself to the renewed importunities of its owner) might be not without imaginative stimulus. Nor might quiet chats with the older among the surrounding peasantry be wholly unproductive. In the short, tomorrow as ever is, I propose to drive over and go on the prowl for copy! I think this entitles me to sign myself, with love,

Your enterprising friend,
PRISCILLA PRINGLE

The writer of this letter was as good as her word – as indeed she ought to have been, since she was actually proposing to herself to be a good deal better. For a plan – let it be announced at once – had formed itself in Miss Pringle's mind.

There are several ways of beginning a reconnaissance in foreign territory of a rural sort. The most common is to discover a sudden need of stamps, and draw up at the village post office. If the post office is the everything-shop as well, so much the better. There will then be three or four female cottagers (as Miss Pringle would have called them) gossiping in the place; these will fall silent as you enter, and then draw aside out of what you may be fond enough to suppose a proper feeling of deference towards the gentry (even foreign gentry); in fact, there has been a sudden outpouring – as of a flood of adrenalin into the bloodstream – of suspicion and hostility of the most primitive sort. But you need not greatly worry about that. This is civilization, after all. The village constable is bedding out lettuces in his garden next door, and (although it wouldn't be his real inclination) he knows that his livelihood depends upon defending you at need. One of the women makes a gesture, indicating that you should jump the queue. They do in fact want to get rid of you, so that they can resume their talk. But you decline, and withdraw modestly into a corner of the constricted space, perhaps affecting to study some faded picture-postcards of local beauty-spots. So the women continue with their miscellaneous purchases, and within a minute they have forgotten about you and resumed their tittle-tattle. Whereupon you listen in. Persons seeking dream cottages, dilapidated and going for a song, but offering the largest scope for inspired modernization, tend to have particular faith in this method of setting to work.

Miss Pringle, however, was not in quest of a hovel, since she was very nicely accommodated in this particular in her own part of the country already. What she sought might be defined as a synoptic view of the social situation in Long Canings and round about. For this reason (but also, of course, because she was a stout churchwoman) she had chosen to present herself at matins in Long Canings church.

For there was still a church in some sort of working order, attended to in such leisure as the pastoral care of the people of Gibber Porcorum afforded the rector of that more populous parish. Miss Pringle had made preliminary inquiries, and she had come over on a Sunday – a pleasantly sunny Sunday – upon which Long Canings was having its innings. As her little car chugged over the last stretch of downland and dropped down to the venerable Wilts and Berks canal, she realized that 'Kandahar', *alias* The Old Rectory, was not going to be hard to find. It dominated the suddenly contracted horizon like a cathedral or a gasometer, and the church in the shade of which it ought modestly to have reposed would in fact have gone into it two or three times over. Apart from a pub and a few scattered cottages of no very prosperous (or even picturesque) appearance, the two structures, moreover, seemed to constitute the totality of the village or hamlet of Long Canings. But this was presently revealed as not quite so. Beyond the church was a shrubbery, beyond the shrubbery was a lawn, and beyond the lawn and on a lower level was a large and rambling – although no-where lofty – manor house put together over some centuries (one had to suppose) to the effect of a careless miscellany of archi-tectural styles. Beyond all this again, and plainly appurtenant to the manor, was a pleasingly imposing park. Miss Pringle, who had a fondness (proper in a lady of good family) for all evidences of spacious and ordered living, felt that she would be much more at home in this squirearchal fastness than in the towering, arched,

41

crocketed, and generally hideous redbrick residence of Captain A. G. de P. Bulkington (also of the Imperial Forces Club, Pall Mall).

The church bell was ringing, monotonously although not quite metronomically, as she drove up. There was nobody in sight, so that when she had parked her car unobtrusively she hastened forward, concluding the congregation to be already assembled within. There was one other car in evidence. Although rakish and secular rather than clerical in cut, its position close to the chancel announced the fact that it had lately embarked the rector of Gibber Porcorum a few miles away and now decanted the rector of Long Canings to perform his subsidiary offices as soon as the bell stopped. In the little churchyard she remarked a large Gloucester Old Spot (not nowadays a fashionable sort of pig) reposed on a flat tomb- stone, and a surprising number of pheasants perched here and there on upright ones. From somewhere near by, but invisible behind a high wall, came the sound of stamping, champing, rattling, snuffling, sneezing and snorting which one associates with a well-populated stableyard.

Composing herself appropriately, Miss Pringle entered the church – and looked round perplexed, since there appeared to be nobody else in the place. But the bell had suddenly stopped, and when she glanced towards the west end (where there was a kind of potting-shed which she knew must lie beneath the tower) it was to become aware that an aged man, rather like a tortoise in a humble walk of reptilian life, had abandoned a dangling rope the better to survey her with what could only be described as offended in- credulity.

'Be you seeking summun?' the tortoise asked.

The question, as addressed to somebody entering a sacred place, was susceptible of a serious interpretation. But Miss Pringle was a little disconcerted.

'I have come to attend matins,' she said. 'Surely – '

'You're early,' the tortoise said morosely – but nevertheless failed to return to his bell. In a religious silence, Miss Pringle sat down. A wooden placard on the wall informed her in barely decipherable lettering that in the year 1604 Jn. Spink, Gent. had donated an unusual sum of 7s. 4d. for the relief of the poor of the parish. An answering placard reminded her that she must not marry her Grandmother's Husband. She became aware of an odd and not displeasing smell as pervading the church, and concluded that the rite of incensation must obtain in it. Olfactory analysis, however, suggested that what was in question could only be a mingling of sundry embrocations, liniments, and saddle-soaps, and must be due to the tortoise's diurnal and secular employment.

Three small girls and a small boy appeared in the choir. The girls stared at Miss Pringle, and then turned to each other, whispering and giggling. The boy also stared at her, but with unrelaxed gravity, and while picking his nose. And then, quite suddenly, the officiating clergyman – doubtless the rector – was advancing from the vestry, with his prayer book held open before him. If one discounted the children (who had small appearance of being capable of serious devotion) and the tortoise (who had sat down at the back of the church and was unfolding a Sunday newspaper), it seemed that Miss Pringle herself was to be the only worshipper.

But this was a false alarm. For now the church door opened – to admit, in the first instance, only the sounds of an indignant female voice, vigorous whackings seemingly delivered with an umbrella or parasol upon a thick hide, and a quick succession of loud protesting squeals. By means which would have distressed St Francis of Assisi, the Gloucester Old Spot was being persuaded of the impropriety of its proposing to attend divine service. The creature could be heard retreating with injured grunts, and its assailant, breathing a little heavily from her just exertions, passed up the aisle and sat down immediately in front of Miss Pringle. She was of about Miss Pringle's age, and her attire attested to a position in the upper ranks of society. Nevertheless, the smell of embrocation and saddle-soap was immediately intensified. Miss Pringle, who was of course a woman of notably acute intelligence, recalled that this region of England was much given to equestrian pursuits.

The door opened again – and Miss Pringle, glancing round, was a shade disconcerted to see that Captain Bulkington had arrived. She had indeed thought it probable that he would be a church-goer, but had envisaged a congregation numerous enough to enable her to escape his observation if she wished to. This was plainly far from being the case; in fact the Captain now sat down within six feet of her, and after placing a bowler hat carefully under the pew proceeded to kneel with great propriety and his familiar creak. And almost immediately it turned out that he was not alone. There was the sound of a second mild disturbance just outside the church; the smack of a stone on stone, a second and duller smack immediately followed by an anguished squeal, a loud laugh and a shout of 'Got him!' from a young and triumphant male voice. Then there entered with complete decorum, and took their places beside the Captain, two youths in impeccable Sunday clothes. They looked round the church, detectably offered each other an expressive glance, and sat back with an air of stoically controlled suffering. Whereupon Captain Bulkington coughed significantly and they tumbled rather lumpishly on their hassocks, conscientiously screwing their eyes very tight meanwhile.

Since these must be pupils (and presumably postulants for the Brigade), Miss Pringle covertly eyed them with a good deal of curiosity. They belonged to contrasting types. One was very tall and very fair, and would no doubt have been handsome in a thoroughly patrician way if he had not also been very weedy (Miss Pringle believed that was the word) and devoid of either a brow or (it seemed) a jaw-bone. The second began like the other (if, that was to say, one started one's inspection from the top), but then quite dramatically diverged from his fellow, since he was more jaw-bone than anything else. Furthermore he was short and burly and his arms seemed unnaturally long. Miss Pringle was almost certain that he must own a lurching gait and bandy legs. The gaze of the first was vacant; and of the second, ferocious. It seemed likely, however, that their common denominator would readily be discovered by an educational psychologist.

But now there was another – and, as it proved, final – incursion of the faithful. A lady of imposing presence swept into the church, exchanged a passing greeting with the embrocation-and-saddle-soap lady, glared stonily at Captain Bulkington and stonily at Miss Pringle, and made her way to a pew of superior pretension immediately in front of the lectern. She was followed by a florid gentleman so patently endowed with Miss Pringle's favourite attribute of perfect diffidence that Miss Pringle was able to tell at once that here was the proprietor of the adjacent mansion which she had glimpsed before entering.

And now the service began.

'Hymn two hundred and three.'
'Hymn three hundred and two.'

The first of these injunctions had been uttered by the rector, and the second – more loudly and not at all diffidently – by the squire. It seemed probable that the squire was right, since a kind of bill of fare depending from a nail near the pulpit declared that 302 it was. Music, approximately organ-like in character, had begun to wheeze encouragingly from somewhere at the back. Miss Pringle wondered whether it was being provided by the tortoise. But a glance assured her that the tortoise was still occupied with his newspaper. So somebody else, charged with the production of this all-important aid to devotion, must somehow have slipped in unobserved.

The situation was a divisive one. The four children in the choir, whose faces now registered a sort of glazed terror, plunged pipingly into 302. The squire and his lady sang 302. The embrocation-woman, who appeared to be tone-deaf, shouted the words of 302. But the rector stuck to 203, and was splendidly supported by Captain Bulkington and his charges. Miss Pringle, finding her sympathies sundered, solved her problem by a silent opening and shutting of the mouth. After this the service ran on smoothly to the First Lesson, in which the squire, rather in the manner of a chairman of companies making an annual report to shareholders, communicated to his auditory various incidents in a battle between Abijah and Jeroboam. And then there was the *Benedicite*.

But at this point a certain amount of disturbance made itself audible from without. In the main it was no more than a matter of the cheerful yelping of small dogs, and Miss Pringle remarked that the congregation took this in its stride. A little puppy-walking was going on in the interest of the local hunt; and it was conceivable that a number of the more polite children in this part of Wiltshire were regularly in the habit of contracting out of the obligation of divine service by undertaking this necessary part of a hunt's activities round about 11 a.m. of a Sunday morning. But if the juvenile hounds hadn't disturbed the worshippers they had certainly disturbed the Gloucester Old Spot, which was making a terrible row. They had also disturbed the pheasants, whose

45

alarmed clack-clacking almost drowned the canticle. Or was it by a sinister pop-popping that the pheasants were disturbed? There could be no question as to the fact. *Somebody* was out shooting *something* – or indeed several persons were. Rabbits? Or was it a pigeon battue? Or were unspeakable ruffians even discharging illicit shot-guns at the sitting pheasants as they perched piously on those tombstones? These questions were clearly agitating the squire. The Gloucester Old Spot panicked; the puppies yelped, sequacious of as yet non-existent foxes; the pheasants clattered and whirred, fearful of leaving their little lives in the air.

But the congregation rose to the challenge, lustily exhorting the whales, the fowls of the air, the beasts and the cattle, to praise their Creator and magnify Him for ever.

And quite soon it was over – because the rector, evidently a sensible man, had decided against a sermon. So the tortoise took round a bag – with a gloomy reserve, but nevertheless as one acknowledging that here at last was an activity which at least made sense – and the rector, having pronounced the benediction, disappeared into the vestry, bearing the alms of the faithful with him. By the time that Miss Pringle had reached the door, however, he had reappeared in a quasi-secular character outside the church porch, clearly for the purpose of conversing with anybody who appeared conversable. But the squire and his lady, together with the embrocation-woman, conscious of having been properly exact in the public discharge of their religious duties, were in full career for the manor house with the air of persons feeling they had earned their sherry. The choir, too, had not stood upon the order of its going; from round a bend in the village street fading but raucous laughter suggested that some wholesome recovery of nerve was going on. This left the organist – an elderly woman, flushed from her exertions, whom Miss Pringle at once distinguished as belonging to some intermediate order of society – together with Captain Bulkington and his pupils, and Miss Pringle herself.

Miss Pringle thus stood in a position of some embarrassment. Probably the rector was as astounded as the tortoise had been at the appearance of a total stranger in his congregation, and only good manners were enabling him to conceal the fact. Miss Pringle, therefore, as she shook hands, felt that it was incumbent upon her to explain herself. But what explanation was she to give? She could hardly announce that she had come to Long Canings in the hope of more precisely acquainting herself with a maniacal streak in the composition of Captain A. G. de P. Bulkington of 'Kandahar'. For one thing, the Captain himself was now standing within a couple of yards of her, with an expression of vague puzzlement on his face. Perhaps he was merely waiting to take a civil farewell of his ghostly counsellor, and to put his pupils through the same obligatory routine. But perhaps he had dimly recognized Miss Pringle, and was determined not to go away until he had recalled where he had seen her before. Miss Pringle was not clear whether or not she wanted the next phase of the affair to inaugurate itself in that way.

'So good of you to come,' the rector was saying, much as if he had been giving a party. 'On such a fine morning, too.'

These might have been judged inane remarks as addressed to a strange sheep which had presented itself, as it were, baaing at the fold. But Miss Pringle was not deceived. Dr Howard (she had now managed to glimpse the name on the church noticeboard) was tall and dark, aquiline and ascetic; he was young rather than middle-aged; and although he hadn't yet been recruited to the higher clergy it seemed probable that this might happen at any time. It was true that he had been a little astray in the matter of that first hymn, but absent-mindedness was probably licensed among bishops, just as it was among professors. Moreover Howard (as Miss Barbara Vanderpump, with her keen historical sense, would have pointed out to her friend at once) was a very grand English surname indeed. Miss Pringle responded to Dr Howard's civilities graciously but unaffectedly. (These would be the words.) 'I have always wanted to see this part of the country,' she added vaguely, 'and I shall take a little run through it this afternoon. I believe you have a most interesting White Horse near Calne.'

'Whites and bays and greys and roans and sorrels,' Dr Howard said unexpectedly. 'And all, it seems, extremely interesting. One hears a great deal about them in these parts. Sir Ambrose' – he made a restrained gesture in the direction of the Big House – 'has whole platoons of them. I always try to find him lessons in which something four-footed is getting around. "He saith to the war-horse 'Ha-ha' " and that sort of thing. You would scarcely believe it, but it livens him up no end. Pity he can't be told to read the hundred and forty-seventh psalm. "He hath no pleasure in the strength of an horse: neither delighteth he in any man's legs." I doubt whether Sir Ambrose would believe his eyes.'

A narrow mind might have found some impropriety in a beneficed clergyman's offering these pleasantries to a stranger. But Miss Pringle was impressed. Dr Howard had an air which made it all seem quite in order. And now he had turned to Bulkington.

'Good morning, Captain,' he said, robustly rather than cordially. 'These young men of yours going to be hunting this season? Cubbing, I suppose, due to start any day now.'

'Hope not, 'pon my soul, padre. Hard work must be the order of the day. Scholarship class, these two, you know. Not a doubt of it. Jenkins, Waterbird – pay your respects to the rector.'

Jenkins and Waterbird, thus admonished, advanced and shook hands with what might have been called – it seemed to Miss Pringle – decently if inexpertly dissimulated hostility. They then stepped backwards, with that ghost of a glance between them.

'Must be getting along,' Captain Bulkington said. 'Set them to a spot of prep before lunch, eh? While Miss Pringle and I have a glass of madeira. Miss Pringle is lunching at the old shop. Can't tempt you to come along, padre?'

'Thank you, but I must get back to Gibber.'

'Too bad. Ready, Miss Pringle? We must be making tracks, then. Things to talk about, eh? Morning to you.'

And Captain Bulkington laid a kindly hand on the elbow of the astonished Miss Pringle, and led her away.

The walk, of course, was a short one – since of an evening, at least, the shadows of the peaked gables of 'Kandahar' must play hide-and-seek among the tombstones through which Miss Pringle was now being conducted. The two young men – for she now realized that neither could be short of nineteen – walked ahead. They seemed to have nothing to say to each other. Their communion, if deep, was of a silent sort.

Chapter Six

Miss Pringle had been taken by surprise. Resolved to spy out the ground unobtrusively before acting (which was Inspector Catfish's habit), she had found herself not a little confused by the bold initiative adopted by her erstwhile travelling-companion. It could not positively be said that, in blandly announcing that she was to lunch with him, Captain Bulkington had not taken an unwarrantable liberty. But then, in proposing this prowl round Long Canings, she had asked for it, after all. The Captain, moreover, was crazed. On just *how* crazed, the feasibility and desirability of the dim plan that had come to her must wholly depend. And the next hour, she felt, would reveal much.

'Is it for the university,' she asked, 'that you are preparing Mr Jenkins and Mr Waterbird?' Conversation had to be made, and this seemed as good a topic as any.

'Certainly. Balliol Scholarships are what I have in mind for them.'

'That is most interesting.' Miss Pringle was perplexed. Her nephew Timothy had been a Scholar of Balliol, and Messrs Jenkins and Waterbird struck her as young men of quite a different sort. But appearances could be deceptive. Captain Bulkington, even though a bit mad, must have some sort of professional experience as a coach. Fond parents, or perplexed trustees, were paying quite a lot for the privilege of sending these youths to 'Kandahar'. They could hardly have failed to make reasonable inquiries about what they were going to get for their money. 'Do you concentrate on that sort of thing?' Miss Pringle asked.

'Lord, no – nothing of the kind. Whatever comes along. Common Entrance, G.C.E. – '

'Quite small boys?'

'If I can get hold of them. Competition fairly keen, you know. But older fellows, as well. Ordination, for instance. There's something in preparing men for that. Serious characters. Dull, I'm afraid. But give no trouble.'

'I see.' Miss Pringle was again perplexed. It was true that

Captain Bulkington had been revealed to her as a devout church-goer. There was something surprising, nevertheless, in the idea of his preparing young men for Holy Orders.

'And then, of course, there's the police. Entrance is very tough there – much tougher than for Balliol – but I take a particular interest in it.'

'As part of your interest in crime?' It was with admirable forth-rightness that Miss Pringle put this question.

'Crime?' Captain Bulkington looked surprised. 'No, no – not an *idée fixe* of mine, 'pon my conscience. Jack of all trades, you might say. Army brings one up to it. Turn your hand to this or that. One moment, though! Give these men their orders. Jenkins, Waterbird!'

'Sir?'

The two young men had turned and spoken on one note. Inanity, indeed, marked the features of Jenkins, and ferocity those of Waterbird. There was something twin-like about them, all the same.

'The principal families of Siena in the sixteenth century. Get them up.'

'We've had that one.' Jenkins spoke helplessly. 'And there's nothing about Siena in the house.'

'Vienna, yes. Siena, no.' Waterbird was warily truculent. 'But Vienna didn't go in for principal families. I looked.'

'Very well.' Captain Bulkington was not disconcerted. '*The Fifteen Decisive Battles of the World.* By Sir Edward Creasy. Distinguished chap. Made a capital judge in India in my grandfather's time. History books, top shelf, far left. Battles three, eight, and twelve, without fail, by six o'clock.' He nodded in a military manner. 'Cut along.'

Jenkins and Waterbird cut. They would have been not unwilling, it seemed to Miss Pringle, to take a swipe at their preceptor as they did so. But they had been brought up, no doubt, to respect their elders and take it out of their juniors instead.

'Ugly louts,' Captain Bulkington said.

'I beg your pardon?' Miss Pringle was startled.

'I said they were nice lads. Come this way. Care to wash? Fetch my housekeeper. Capital woman – has all that at her finger-tips. And then we'll settle down to our chat.'

*

'Time for a peg, eh?' In what he referred to as his sanctum Captain Bulkington was standing before a well-appointed tray. 'Brandy and soda? Brandy and belattee pawnee, we used to say. Can't remember why. Tamil, perhaps. Or was it Teligu? Recollection not too strong on all that.'

'I believe you mentioned madeira.' Brandy before lunch was, to Miss Pringle's mind, definitely an indulgence for gentlemen.

'To be sure. Here it is. And now, my dear, about out little project.' The Captain, as he made use of this startlingly familiar form of address, thrust a glass into Miss Pringle's hand, and waved her to a chair. 'Deuced glad you've come round to it. Have a lot of fun, eh? Cunning ways of going about the thing. That's what we're after. Put our heads together.'

'The thing?' Miss Pringle had been at once thrilled and startled by what she judged to be a maniacal glint in Captain Bulkington's eye. 'Murder?'

'Murder?' The Captain was a little doubtful. 'Rather gone off that, as a matter of fact. Not much money in it, if you ask me. What I've been thinking about is kidnapping. What would you say to that?'

'Kidnapping?' Miss Pringle felt a momentary sense of disappointment, which no doubt betrayed itself in her tone. Infirmity of purpose in Captain Bulkington must be countered, if anything at all was to come of her grand design. This interview had taken her by surprise, and it was only slowly that her mind was becoming at all clear on what ought to be her line. But she saw it now. Captain Bulkington's promisingly criminal vision must be encouraged and – so to speak – canalized. 'I'm afraid,' Miss Pringle said, 'that kidnapping wouldn't interest me very much. I'd scarcely consider myself competent to work out anything of the kind, or to give you an effective hand at it. Murder is another matter. I could put you on the rails there.'

'Ha, ha! Deuced odd conversation this, eh? Our just thinking about writing book, I mean.' Captain Bulkington was suddenly looking at Miss Pringle with broad and unspeakable guile. 'But we understand each other, wouldn't you say?'

'I am sure we do.' Miss Pringle was a little surprised by the effect of dark double-meaning she had contrived to lend these simple words.

'And you are the expert, my dear. I shall be delighted to work at murder, if that's how you feel. Just a matter of finding the right victim, and going ahead. Or victims, for that matter. What about Jenkins and Waterbird? Much to be said for murdering *them*.' The Captain frowned, as if conscious of having gone rather badly off the rails. 'Very jolly fellows, eh? Good families, too.' He paused, and shot a sharp glance at Miss Pringle. 'Pinkerton, now – what would you say to him?'

'Pinkerton?'

'Sir Ambrose. Fellow who read the lessons. Baronet, and all that. We might well think of Pinkerton.'

'As somebody to be murdered?'

'Or kidnapped. Bound to say my mind comes back to that.'

'But what would be the point of kidnapping Sir Ambrose?' Not surprisingly, Miss Pringle's head was beginning to swim.

'Give him a bad time.' Captain Bulkington's reply was alarmingly prompt. 'And his wife would be no good. Nobody would give twopence to get *her* back.'

Miss Pringle restrained an impulse to rise and bolt. Of Captain Bulkington's substantial madness there could now be no doubt whatever. He existed, as Barbara Vanderpump had averred, in a dream of unachieved crimes. Whether this could be called a hopeful circumstance, Miss Pringle was by no means sure. *He is a dreamer* – she almost heard herself saying with Julius Caesar – *Let us leave him: pass*. But one couldn't be certain. His bite *might* be as bad as his bark. Miss Pringle (who was already becoming the victim of her own splendid imagination) thought it was worth continuing to take a chance on.

'For the moment,' she said, 'let us stick to the central fact. Sir Ambrose is to be your victim. He is going to be killed, and the killer is going to get away with it. But just who – I mean, what sort of person – is going to commit the crime? Have you at all thought, for instance, of somebody rather like yourself?' Miss Pringle's voice was more loaded than ever; transparent conspiratorial irony positively clotted it.

'Ha-ha-ha!' Captain Bulkington laughed so loud and long that Captain Bulkington's housekeeper, a respectable female, stuck her head through the door of the sanctum, and then withdrew it again. 'Capital joke, that. Matter of fact, my mind has been moving towards Miss Anketel. Playing around her, you might say. What would you say to her?'

'I'm afraid I've never heard of Miss Anketel.' Miss Pringle was bewildered. 'Is she a friend of yours?'

'Woman who sat in front of you in church. Thick with the Pinkertons, as a matter of fact. And then there's the parson, Henry Howard. He ought to come in. Up your street, that. *Ratsbane in the Rectory*, eh?'

This was not, as it happened, the title of one of Miss Pringle's romances of the clergy, but the Captain's use of it showed that he at least remembered the general character of her work. She sipped her madeira, and wondered whether it would be wise to stay to lunch. Perhaps she should escape; make her way to, say, that interesting White Horse at Calne; and try a little to think things out. Perhaps she ought to call the whole thing off. Any joint enterprise (if that was how to think of it) undertaken with Captain Bulkington was revealing itself as something to which considerable hazards must attach.

'Kidnapping *and* murder!' the Captain said suddenly. 'A double bill, so to speak. How about that?'

'It deserves to be considered, certainly,' Miss Pringle said, rather desperately. 'And we might even go further. Arson could be got in, too. And a little forgery. Embezzlement, for that matter.'

'Arson's quite an idea.' Captain Bulkington, as he absent-mindedly poured himself more brandy, was plainly pondering deeply. 'Yes, arson attracts me. The Hall, eh?'

'The Hall?'

'Pinkerton's place. A pretentious bounder, Pinkerton. Amusing to see the flames licking round him, you think, my dear? A great crackling and roaring there would be, as well as a howling, if one managed a really healthy blaze. Yes, I like that. Not so sure about forgery and what's-its-name. A shade tame, to my mind. For our readers, that's to say.'

There was no doubt that an hour *was* revealing much. The psychology, or rather the psychopathology, of Captain Bulkington was coming, indeed, alarmingly clear. He seemed not to be a mercenary man. It was true that his devotion to the cause of higher education could be felt as rather a bread-and-butter affair. But every man, after all, has to find a livelihood, and coaching youths and boys was a perfectly honourable means to that end. And his original suggestion to Miss Pringle, although cock-eyed, had not been economically motivated; indeed, he had rather suggested that he was prepared to pay £500 for the fun of having a go at a mystery story and seeing his name in print. But the obverse of all this was disturbing. What compelled the fancy of the Captain on its more morbid side was not any sort of crime that came along; it was decidedly what the law calls crime against the person. The image of Sir Ambrose Pinkerton – surely a blameless enough landed proprietor – howling amid the flames of his collapsing mansion was a shade daunting to one of Miss Pringle's natural refinement of mind. Collaboration with Captain Bulkington, even although she was proposing to construe 'collaboration' in a private and somewhat Pickwickian sense, would require a good deal of finesse. In particular, it would require delicate timing in the final phase of the affair.

'Captain Bulkington,' Miss Pringle asked with some formality, 'have you considered what means we might take to launch this joint enterprise?'

'Suggest you move in here.' The Captain's reply was prompt and confident. 'Free bed and board, eh?' He laughed robustly, apparently unaware that his collaborator had judged his form of words to verge on the indelicate. 'And I dare say you wouldn't mind lending a hand with some of the men? Jenkins and Waterbird, for instance. Good for them to have a mature woman about the place. Take their minds off the village girls.'

'Initially, at least, I judge that it would be best to proceed differently.' Miss Pringle was not sure how she regarded being described as a mature woman, nor whether she altogether relished being envisaged as a socially elevating factor in the libidinous fantasies of Captain Bulkington's young men. But she was quite clear that she was not prepared to suffer domestication in 'Kandahar'. 'I suggest that we correspond. That seems to me the best means of discovering whether something can be worked out.' Miss Pringle rose on this vague note. 'And it has been so kind of you to ask me to stay to lunch. Unfortunately, I have an engagement with a clerical cousin who lives near Lechlade.' Like all novelists, Miss Pringle believed in making her lies circumstantial. 'A Rural Dean. A most charming man.'

'Aha! Out for a bit of copy, eh? *Death at the Deanery*. Only do Rural Deans have Deaneries? I don't believe they do.' To Miss Pringle's surprise, Captain Bulkington appeared unoffended by her abrupt intimation of departure. He led her to the door of the sanctum. 'Write each other letters, you mean, about whatever dodges we either of us think up?'

'It is something of that sort that is in my mind.'

'Capital! Bound to say I hadn't thought of it. But it might fit very well.' Captain Bulkington paused to rub his hands – a gesture which Miss Pringle had not observed him to perform before. 'The very thing, my dear. Deuced clever suggestion.' There was something like a new glint in the Captain's eye. 'And the sooner we begin the better.'

'No doubt. But there is one condition which, I suggest, must be observed.' Miss Pringle glanced a shade warily at her private madman (for it was thus that she was coming to think of the Captain). 'The postal service – particularly in country areas such as we both live in – is not always reliable. In point of confidentiality, I mean.'

'Confidentially? Prying eyes, steaming letters open and so forth? Perfectly true.'

'In our conversation, Captain Bulkington, we have been led into talking at times almost as if we were contemplating *real* crime –'

'Good Lord!' The Captain looked much shocked. 'But you're entirely right. Extraordinary thing.'

'A mere shorthand, of course.'

'Just that. You express it deuced well.'

'A *façon de parler*, in fact.'

'Quite so, quite so.' The Captain sounded a little vague on this one. 'So you would suggest –'

'My own letters will be strictly about the writing of a book. And I have no doubt that your own' – and Miss Pringle bent upon the Captain what in print she would have described as a subtly ironical regard – 'I have no doubt that your own will observe a similar discretion.'

'Not a doubt about it. Bear it in mind. Damned good tip. Comes of being a pro.' Captain Bulkington's admiration had drawn him into even more than commonly staccato utterance. 'All plain sailing, eh?'

'I certainly hope so.'

'And about the money, now. Remember some mention of £500, my dear? Would that be about right, if we brought the thing off?'

'For the mere technical know-how for a single simple murder,' Miss Pringle said with gruesome facetiousness, 'it would be a most adequate remuneration.'

The accomplices (as they might whimsically have been called) now made their way into the garden of 'Kandahar', and thereafter the Captain courteously proposed to escort his visitor to the front gate.

'Where shall we begin?' he asked.

'With the outline of a story turning on arson, I suppose, since you tell me you have taken a fancy to that.'

'Arson *and* murder.' Captain Bulkington was emphatic. 'And – do you know? – I think we might have at least a dodge or two in the murdering way first. Yes – I think I'd feel happier with that.'

'Then so be it,' Miss Pringle said composedly. And she shook hands graciously, and returned to her car.

Chapter Seven

It had been a tiring morning, however, and Captain Bulkington's madeira hadn't really taken her very far. At Lechlade (near which lived a mythical Rural Dean) there was no doubt a hotel and the prospect of a substantial lunch. But here in Long Canings she had noticed a pub – no more than a pot-house, but bound to respond to a robust call for bread and cheese and a half-pint of bitter. Moreover it bore rather a mysterious name – the Jolly Chairman – and she was always attracted by mysteries. So why not drop in? She might even pick up some useful gossip from the locals as they tanked up before their Sunday dinner. Something of the sort had been, after all, part of her original plan of campaign.

Miss Pringle turned away from her car, and walked over to this promising hostelry.

She chose the public rather than the saloon bar, for she was a woman who knew the ropes in such matters. Four village lads were playing darts, and two of them were so young that a magistrate would certainly have frowned upon their frequenting licensed premises. But she knew that in such trivial matters the rule of law does not always obtain in places like Long Canings, since a just entitlement to free beer is attractive to village constables. There was, of course, the graver point of Sabbath Observance, upon which Miss Pringle commonly held unbending views. The darts ought to be locked up. But in the interest of the serious investigation upon which she was engaged it might be reasonable to disregard this.

The tortoise was also present. A solitary man, he was engaged in feeding sixpences into a fruit machine, tugging the handle, and then standing back to stare at the consequent gyrations of the silly little symbols with morose indifference. Miss Pringle, whose modest order was being quite civilly attended to by the man behind the bar, wondered whether the tortoise could be coaxed into conversation. But a suitable initial topic eluded her. Their common ground, after all, was singularly limited; it might be said to consist of a sermon that hadn't been preached and two or three hymns so execrably sung that no sane person would want to recall them. She was about to turn her attention to the youths playing darts when the bar door opened and Messrs Jenkins and Waterbird walked in.

Or rather they made to walk in, hesitated, and then *did* walk in. The hitch had presumably been occasioned by Miss Pringle, whom they hadn't expected to see. Or had they? Miss Pringle, professionally acute in the reading of small appearances, found that she wasn't sure. Had they followed her from 'Kandahar' out of idle curiosity? Had they made her a subject of ribald talk – and then had the decency a little to falter when thus impertinently once more in her presence? However this might be, she was not going to show herself put out. There might be information to be extracted from them of a more reliable order than from the tattle of rustics. And it might be amusing, at least, a little to take the wind out of their sails.

'So we meet again!' Miss Pringle called out cheerfully. 'It must be to allow me to take the privilege of my years.' And she laughed what she thought of as a sporting-aunt type of laugh. 'What would you care to drink?'

Mr Jenkins (who was the fair and chinless youth) merely let his mouth gape open a little, like a fish feeling a sudden need to extract an extra ration of oxygen from its tank. But Mr Waterbird (who on the other hand might have been proposing to seize and savagely shake the bars of his cage) had more presence of mind.

'Large gin and small tonic,' he said briskly. 'And a large tonic and a small gin for the boy.' And at this he in his turn laughed so heartily that the tortoise turned round to stare, a sixpence held suspended in his hand. Then, quite abruptly, this simian youth changed, as it were, his *persona*, and became the best type of English public school boy. 'I don't think we were really introduced,' he said, producing a modest smile. 'This is my friend Ralph Jenkins. And I'm Adrian Waterbird.'

'How do you do? My name is Priscilla Pringle.' Miss Pringle paused for a moment then, finding Mr Ralph Jenkins apparently indisposed to emend his companion's facetious suggestion, ordered the gin and tonics as proposed. 'Why,' she inquired humorously, when the drinks appeared, 'are you not both buys with those decisive battles of the world?'

'We nipped out on the quiet,' Adrian said. 'Ralph, that's right?'

'We nipped out,' Ralph agreed with a gulp.

'It's all we can do. Treated rather like kids, you see. Ralph?'

'All we can do,' Ralph said hastily. 'Kids. That's it.'

'I say, Miss Pringle – shall we all go and sit outside? Quieter. I'll carry your sandwiches. We've got half an hour before lunch.' Adrian was already holding open the door. 'It's nice to have somebody to talk to. The old Bulgar doesn't have many visitors.'

'The old Bulgar?' Miss Pringle echoed. She hoped that she had accurately heard the word.

'Our name for Captain Bulkington. I think Bulgars are the same as Tartars, more or less.' Adrian had produced this ethnographical statement with confidence. 'And he's that, all right. Ralph?'

'That's right. He's an old – ' Ralph seemed a little at sea. 'Jolly day,' he said hastily. 'A shame not to be outside.'

There was an unkempt garden at the side of the inn, with a few benches and tables, and untenanted except for a dog dismally clanking its chain beside a kennel. They all sat down. Miss Pringle found herself pinning a good deal of hope on the gin – even on the inane Ralph's small one. She was conscious of being still undesirably short of facts. And particularly of one large psychological fact. How harmless was Captain Bulkington? If complete harmlessness was his true token, she told herself, he was really going to be no use to her at all. Of course, if he was dangerous she would have to look out for herself. He might be precisely that to her. But she was a courageous woman. And in the interest of the mighty thought that had come to her she was prepared for a certain amount of risk. Some sense of the character of her hopeful collaborator was the first thing to get hold of. And these two odd young men were living with him in what must be a quite uncomfortable degree of intimacy. It was true they were not clever (although she was not quite sure about the anthropoid yet protean Adrian Waterbird). Nevertheless they must have their view.

'Does Captain Bulkington work you very hard?' she asked conversationally.

'He certainly does,' Adrian said decidedly. 'He has the edge on us, you see. Ralph?'

'That's it!' There were signs of Ralph's being suddenly prompted to voluble speech. 'You see, he found out – '

'Shut up, Ralph, and drink your kindergarten drench.' Adrian's more polite manner had momentarily vanished. 'It's just that the Bulgar has got our people – my father and Ralph's guardian – taped. Our last chance, and so on. I get through this rotten exam, or I'm booked for New South Wales. You see, my family has some property there. But I don't know anything about it. Full of blacks, I expect.' Adrian shook his head gloomily. 'As for Ralph, he's going to be put in a bicycle factory.'

'Push-bikes,' Ralph said. 'Kids' tricycles, too, they say.' He, perhaps in imitation of his dominant friend, also shook a gloomy head. 'It's bloody murder.'

'Murder?' For a moment Miss Pringle was startled. Then she recovered herself. 'You have some alternative career in mind, Mr Jenkins?' It sometimes pleased Miss Pringle to be a mistress of delicate irony.

'I wouldn't mind doing the Monte Carlo Rally. Or the Monaco Grand Prix. But here we are instead.' Ralph's vacant stare for a moment hinted helpless perplexity. 'The fact is, we haven't had a hope since the Bulgar found out – '

'Ralph maunders,' Adrian said. 'The worst part of it is, you see, that we don't really think Bulkington is a proper coach at all. Or I don't. Thinking isn't much Ralph's line.'

'Do you mean,' Miss Pringle asked as if with mild interest, 'that the establishment at "Kandahar" is simply a cover for some other activity?'

'I suppose it might be put that way.' Adrian had now absorbed most of his double gin, but its only effect was to superimpose what might have been a look of cunning on the alarming ferocity which his habitual expression suggested. 'Certainly his mind is on other things. Perhaps he was quite a good crammer long ago. But I've decided he knows next to nothing about the job as it is now. That stuff about decisive battles, for instance. It's completely old-hat. He might as well have told us to go out and clean the windows, like the schoolmaster in Scott's novel.'

'Dickens's,' Miss Pringle said.

'All right, Dickens's. And this business of saying he's preparing us for something or other at Oxford. It seems that as things are there nowadays, that's just false pretences.' Adrian Waterbird removed the slice of lemon from his glass, and for a moment sucked it sombrely. 'Ralph ran into his old housemaster last holidays, and told him about the Balliol Scholarship thing. The chap just roared with laughter.'

'How very rude and unkind.'

'It was candid, anyway. Ralph?'

'That's right – candid. He said the Bulgar must be a madman.' Ralph fished out his own piece of lemon. 'I said no – just a maniac.'

'A maniac!' Miss Pringle exclaimed.

'Well, yes.' Adrian chucked his scrap of lemon expertly at the chained dog, catching it in the eye. 'We think you ought to know. And we think you ought to keep away. It's all right for men. We can take it. Even Ralph can take it. But it wouldn't be at all nice for a lady, if you ask me.'

'We think you oughtn't to take it,' Ralph Jenkins said.

'To *take* it?'

'Well, the job. Doesn't the Bulgar want to hire you for something? That's been our guess.'

Miss Pringle was obliged to reflect that it wasn't a bad guess. Circumspection, however, was required.

'There is no question of anything that could be called employment,' she said with dignity. 'But Captain Bulkington and I have had a little business to discuss. May I ask just what sort of maniac you suppose him to be?'

'A homicidal maniac, of course.' Adrian seemed surprised. 'Ralph and I are pretty sure he did in the last chap.'

'The last chap?' Any undue excitement, Miss Pringle hoped, was absent from her voice. But, of course, she *was* excited. Here, at least, were two independent witnesses who believed Captain Bulkington to be not a mere visionary but the real thing. 'Who was the last chap?'

'The crammer the Bulgar took over from, of course.'

'But Captain Bulkington's predecessor in "Kandahar" – who I do happen to know met some sinister end – was a clergyman. In fact he was the rector of Long Canings, and the house was the rectory.'

'Yes, I know.' Adrian Waterbird glanced into his almost empty glass. 'Can I get you another half pint of that beer?' he asked.

'No, thank you.'

'Then I'll just freshen this up a bit. Half as much again, you know. That's a very good rule when drinking.' Having offered this serious adult communication, Adrian rose and made for the bar. There *was* something ape-like in his gait, Miss Pringle reflected. She was almost surprised to be surveying a pair of well-tailored pin-stripe trousers and not a purple and orange behind.

'Adrian will be a drunk a damn sight sooner than he'll be a B.A.' This was the first independent observation Ralph Jenkins had offered. 'But an old bastard like the Bulgar would drive anybody to the bottle. The way he got us just where he wants us – not even daring to write home about the bloody farce of his silly battles and all that – it was a trap, if you ask me.'

'A trap?'

'He planted her on us. Probably paid her thirty bob for the job. And then in he came.'

'I'm afraid I don't understand you, Mr Jenkins.'

'That's just as well.' Mr Jenkins was eyeing with alarm the unexpectedly quick return of Mr Waterbird from the bar. 'It's not a thing for ladies, at all. And please don't tell Adrian I got going on it. It's not in what he calls our terms of reference.'

'Your terms of reference? Whatever do you mean by that?'

'I really don't know.' And Ralph favoured Miss Pringle with his most inane and helpless stare. 'It's all a bit deep, you see. I can't say I'm really with it.'

'It sounds as if that may be just as well.' Miss Pringle was aware that she had been shown the tip of something highly discreditable – and not of an order which would be of any use to her in her fastidious fiction. She therefore dismissed it from her mind, and turned to the advancing Adrian. There was quite a lot of something in his replenished glass, but nevertheless the small tonic bottle in his other hand was full. 'Will you tell me a little more,' she said, 'about Captain Bulkington's coming to "Kandahar"?'

'Yes, of course.' Adrian sat down again. 'You don't happen to have any cigarettes?'

'I believe I have.' Miss Pringle produced a packet from her bag.

'Thanks a lot.' Adrian took a cigarette, and Miss Pringle made a professional note inside her head. She had been mistaken, it appeared, in supposing that this idiom could be employed only in the representation of lower-class conversation. 'He keeps us so bloody short, you see.' Adrian took a gulp of what he had already had enough of. 'And – by the way – I'm afraid the barman will be coming out for his money. Do you mind? What the Bulgar calls my allowance was all blued on beer by Wednesday.'

'I don't mind at all.' Miss Pringle did her best to feel amused. 'But about Captain Bulkington's arrival,' she said, 'and the mysterious event upon which it succeeded.'

'The point is that this black beetle – '

'This what?'

'This rector chap. He took pupils, you see. Poor sods just like Ralph and me. It was quite the thing in those days. You took up the Church, and found the pay-packet was about zero. So you got up a bit of Greek again – and no doubt those fifteen battles as well – and announced in *The Times* or somewhere that at the rectory, Long Canings, pupils would be received, enrolled, and prepared for entrance to either of the universities. That's the Bulgar's formula still. "Enrolled" is what's important. It commits the poor sucker – the fond parent, that is – to paying up.'

'I have no doubt it does.' When in liquor, Miss Pringle remarked to herself, Mr Waterbird was still not quite what could be thought of as a Balliol man. But he expressed his views more resourcefully than seemed compatible with a completely moronic mind. 'Please go on.'

'The Bulgar came in as an assistant. What we used to call an usher, where I went to school. And then he worked himself up, or in. He hadn't a bean of his own. Somebody had got him a commission in a decent regiment, but they'd turfed him out for cheating at cards. Probably it was at baccarat.'

'This is most interesting, Mr Waterbird. But may I ask how you come to know about it?'

'Oh, that's a long story.' Mr Waterbird produced this dismissive phrase with confidence. 'Anyway, he got together just a little. Probably he ran the alms-house – there *was* an alms-house – and screwed it out of the almsmen's porridge. Just enough to buy up the goodwill of the cramming racket after he'd rubbed out the rector.'

'And just *how* did he rub out the rector?'

'That's a long story too. Probably much as he plans to rub out Sir Ambrose.'

'As *what*?'

'It's an obsession with him. He pretty well can't think of anything else. I'm surprised you can have had any conversation with him without its all tumbling out.'

Chapter Eight

The normally steady head of Miss Priscilla Pringle was reeling – and it wasn't from beer. Adrian Waterbird had said the most extraordinary things, and her first impulse was to demand, as it were, chapter and verse for them; to require him to back up his unprompted and heartening assertion about Captain Bulkington's lethal designs upon his neighbour Sir Ambrose Pinkerton with a decent amount of corroborative detail. Then she suddenly saw that nothing of the kind would by any means do.

She mustn't take this conversation seriously. She must adopt the line – or be prepared at a future date to adopt the line – that these boys talked light-hearted nonsense which simply wouldn't stick in one's head. That she had received any responsible or persuasive or memorable opinion to the effect that the Captain was potentially a dangerous criminal might put her in a very delicate situation in certain circumstances which she envisaged later on. And there was a corollary to this. *She must stop fishing around.* Unless Messrs Jenkins and Waterbird were shocking young liars – or dwellers in an infantile fantasy world – she now knew as much as she needed to know. It would be awkward, of course, if throughout Long Canings and beyond it was soberly known to all men that Captain Bulkington had once killed a rector and now proposed to kill a baronet. But not too awkward, provided she quickly reduced her own communications with the place to a minimum. She would be able to maintain that she had simply happened never to hear a breath of these suspicions; that the Captain existed for her only as an agreeable if slightly eccentric acquaintance who had taken an odd fancy to collaborate with an acknowledged expert in the fabricating of a little detective fiction. That must be her public line all through. Her satisfactory knowledge that he was authentically a bizarre public menace with nothing but sensational headlines at the end of his road: this she must keep to herself.

Miss Pringle picked up her bag. It was extremely fortunate that she had so firmly told Captain Bulkington that their project was, for a time at least, to be furthered only by epistolary correspondence. Until the climax of her dimly discerned grand design, Long Canings had better not see her again. Captain Bulkington must, so to speak, be led up the garden path by remote control.

As she stood up, she looked appraisingly at Adrian Waterbird. (To expend appraisal on Ralph Jenkins would be absurd.) The barman, it occurred to her, would be obliged at a pinch to testify that the young gentleman with the glare and the scowl and the jaw had fairly rapidly consumed two large gins. After that, very little credence would be accorded to what Adrian said he had said. (And Ralph in a witness-box would be more tragi-comedy.)

'You boys must have great fun together,' Miss Pringle announced, reverting to her jolly-aunt note. 'You say anything that comes into your heads. And now I must be off. I hope that you are both deservedly successful in your examinations, and that New South Wales and the bicycle factory become no more than uncertainly remembered threats. And our memories *are* mercifully selective. For instance, we have had a most amusing talk, but one having nothing to do with the serious business of life. It will have vanished from my head tomorrow morning – which I hope won't be true of your grip of Sir Edward Creasy's Battles three, eight, and twelve. Good-bye.'

And Miss Pringle shook hands. She was rather pleased with this parting speech. Ralph Jenkins had, of course, merely gaped at it. But Adrian Waterbird, she thought, had for a moment gaped too.

It was in the middle of Gibber Porcorum – if Gibber Porcorum could be said to have a middle – that one of Miss Pringle's front tyres collapsed with an old-fashioned bang. She drew up beside a hedge, got out, and surveyed the mischief. The nail was plain to see. She supposed, although the point was irrelevant to her plight, that it had come out of a horse-shoe. And out of a horse, for that matter. As a child Miss Pringle had often watched and sniffed while the blacksmith was at work. His had appeared a most barbaric craft, but the horses didn't seem to mind. Horses are less sensitive to nails than are motor-cars.

Miss Pringle was conscious of an irrational unease. She wanted to get safely back to Worcestershire – where she could think again, and decide whether or not to embark upon a first preceptorial letter to Captain Bulkington. She wanted, at least for the present, no more encounters with Captain Bulkington's circle; she wanted to get away from what her friend Miss Vanderpump would have called his *ambiance*.

But this was not to be.

'Hullo! Can I be of any help?' It was the rector of Gibber Porcorum (and Long Canings) who spoke – and from over the hedge in the shade of which Miss Pringle's car reposed. It was the rectory hedge, and Dr Howard was trimming it in what was no doubt a perfectly proper employment for a clergyman on a Sunday afternoon.

'Thank you,' Miss Pringle said, and was about to add: 'I can perfectly easily change a wheel myself'. But this is something which a lady may not roundly say to a gentleman without the imputation of an aggressive feminism. This is unfair, but it remains a social fact. It can be said, of course, to a husband, brother, or nephew, but not to any other male (except, perhaps, to an officious tramp).

'Thank you,' Miss Pringle repeated, 'but I really mustn't trouble you. I am sure there is a garage close by.'

'There is nothing of the kind.' Dr Howard dropped his shears, strode to his garden gate, and vaulted it. The ease of this performance made it perfectly clear that pushing a diminutive car around was something that would afford him no trouble at all. 'Have you got a jack,' he asked briskly, 'or shall I fetch mine?'

'It's in the boot.' Miss Pringle was constrained to accept the role of helpless female with a good grace. 'The spare is properly blown up. I always see to that.'

'Wise virgin,' Dr Howard said.

Miss Pringle discerned that her rescuer was disposed to prize the natural authority which enabled him to say anything that came into his head. His was an unassuming station within the Anglican Church. But he was, in the metaphorical sense of the term, a large man – and he genuinely possessed that aristocratic quality which she had once, in a railway compartment, so mistakenly attributed to Captain A. G. de P. Bulkington. This didn't make her any the more willing to have much conversation with him now.

'I thought you were lunching with Bulkington,' Dr Howard said.

'That was a misunderstanding, I had other plans.'

'You must be uncommonly hungry by this time. Or have you had something to eat?'

'Thank you. I had a substantial sandwich at the Jolly Chairman.' Miss Pringle made this awkward admission only because she had been in fear of being led into the rectory, regaled on cold roast beef and pickles, and peremptorily questioned the while.

'Just pull on the handbrake now, will you?' There could be no doubt of Dr Howard's expertness as a mechanic. 'No damage to the wall of the tyre, I think. You pulled up pretty quick. Smart girl.'

The rector was much too young thus to address Miss Pringle with any propriety. But since it was a long time since anybody had so addressed her she accepted this venturesomeness with a laugh.

'By the way,' Dr Howard said, 'I know who you are, and I've enjoyed some of your stories. But they're busman's holidays, rather, so far as I'm concerned. Why not get away from all those parsons for a time? Write a story about somebody like Bulkington. There's plenty of scope there.' Dr Howard tapped the spare wheel firmly on its studs. 'There, and in Long Canings in general. Or any

English village, for that matter. Homicidal feeling in every hall and hovel, court and cottage, manor and – '

'I make it a rule,' Miss Pringle interrupted with some severity, 'in no circumstances to take as a starting-point for fiction anyone who has come within the range of my own acquaintance.'

'That can't be other than nonsense, you know. You can't begin from the moon. But perhaps you just take your characters from other people's books?'

'I do nothing of the kind.' Miss Pringle was intelligent enough to see a weak argumentative position in front of her. 'Of course one writes from one's own experiences. But the imagination, Dr Howard, is always at work. It is a deep, transforming power. Of course actual people – people one has known – play their part. But they sink down, you must understand, into the deep well of unconscious cerebration, to come up transformed. One begins to write on the basis of this transformed material. So there can be no question of actual portraiture.'

'That is very reassuring. I've always thought, incidentally, that real portraits must be much more difficult than fancy ones. That was certainly true of drawing and painting when one was a child, and tried to do Daddy or Mummy, and not just a pirate or a high-wayman. So perhaps it's a factor in work like yours.'

'It may be so.' Miss Pringle again spoke a little stiffly, since she was uncertain that she wasn't being laughed at. 'Ought I to get out the pump?'

'Quite unnecessary. The spare is fully inflated, as you said. I just have to tighten the nuts. Did you encounter anybody interesting in the Jolly Chairman?'

'It was far from busy.' Miss Pringle hesitated. Was this a trap? That we weave for ourselves a tangled web when first we practise to deceive was something which she suddenly had an ominous premonition as possibly to be proved on her own pulse. But she was (it must be reiterated) a courageous woman, and she would not lightly turn back. 'The two young men I met after matins were there. I think they are among Captain Bulkington's pupils? I didn't catch their names.'

'Among his pupils? Well, not exactly. As far as I know, they're the only two he's got. Money in them, though. Wealthy families. Adrian Waterbird is a Shropshire Waterbird.' Dr Howard paused to chuckle at what might have been an odd piece of ornithological information. 'And Ralph Jenkins's father manufactures something or other in a really big way.'

'Indeed? I didn't much attend to them.' Miss Pringle hesitated, and then proceeded against her own better sense of caution. 'You seem to believe in knowing about your parishioners.'

'I shouldn't be much of a country parson if I didn't. Even the casuals, Miss Pringle. I like to get to know a little about them.'

'I see you are referring to me as in that odd category.' Miss Pringle laughed a laugh rather in Miss Vanderpump's silvery manner. 'And you know a little about me already.'

'The jack can come out now. When I saw you in my congregation – and recognized you from those photographs – I told myself you must be doing field work.'

'Field work, Dr Howard?'

'Collecting copy, as they say. Not that you mustn't have done enough of that long ago. For I take it you are a daughter of the vicarage?'

'My dear father was an Archdeacon,' Miss Pringle said with dignity. 'And as for my purpose in attending – '

'Yes, of course.' Dr Howard glanced at Miss Pringle with a horridly justified scepticism. 'But what about those two lads? Mightn't you make something of them? After they'd been down in that deep well of unconscious cerebration, of course. Did they get talking about the Bulgar?'

'The Bulgar?' There was a convincing blank bewilderment in Miss Pringle's voice.

'Their name for Bulkington. Talking of deep wells, by the way, my predecessor at Long Canings abruptly ended his days in one. It occurred to me during the *Benedicite* that you might have heard about that.'

'Nothing of the kind. And I should have supposed that your mind – '

'Perfectly true. But my thoughts do culpably stray at times during a service. I'm sure it's not something that ever happens in one's congregation. There! You're fit for the road again. Shall you be home in time for evensong?'

He *was* laughing at her – and in a manner, surely, that ill befitted his cloth. But Miss Pringle found that, though perturbed, she was not indignant. There was something rather exciting about Dr Howard. She wondered why so masculine and handsome a man wasn't married. He had a vocation for celibacy, perhaps. If so, it seemed a pity.

'Thank you very much, indeed,' she said, as she climbed into the driving seat of her car. 'It has been most kind of you. And I hope I haven't too much delayed your work on that beautiful hedge. Gibber Porcorum is a delightful place. I shall always remember it.'

'Either here or at Long Canings' – Dr Howard was suddenly decorously conventional – 'we are always glad to welcome visitors.'

'That is something very nice to know.' And Miss Pringle extended a gracious hand, let in the clutch, and drove away.

Chapter Nine

In fact our heroine stood not upon the order of her going, but went at once. And this proved to be a mistake, since her more haste ended in the less speed. The road out of Gibber Porcorum was less a road than a lane; it wound; it ran between high banks. Rounding a bend with her foot a little too confidently on the accelerator, Miss Pringle received a confused impression of imminent collision with a large brown mass, and pulled up with her bonnet sited alarmingly and grotesquely beneath the hindquarters of a horse.

The horse had pulled up too. Miss Pringle, calling out words of apology (for the horse had a rider), put her car abruptly into reverse. The horse screamed in agony. The rider swore. Miss Pringle, who hadn't even known that horses *could* scream, or even that a lady (for the rider was a lady) could swear quite like *that*, managed to arrest her retrograde progress just before the brute would have been brought sprawling to the ground. The disastrous truth was evident. Incredibly, the greater part of its tail had got itself tangled in her radiator.

Lady Pinkerton, who had looked at Miss Pringle stonily in church, was looking at her stonily now. That she was doing this from the saddle made the effect the more intimidating. But at least she had stopped uttering those quite shocking imprecations. She seemed, indeed, to be going through the process known as choosing one's words.

'Who are you?' Lady Pinkerton asked.

This is a question, inoffensive in many tones and contexts, into which much arrogance can be stuffed. Lady Pinkerton had stuffed it. And Miss Pringle instantly reflected – for she was a woman of swift-moving mind – that if Sir Ambrose Pinkerton's diffident air so much belied him that he was at all like his wife, then the lethal feelings and intentions of Captain Bulkington had a good deal to be said for them. She decided, however, to ignore the unmannerly question flung at her.

'I am afraid,' she said politely, 'that you will be obliged to dismount. Your horse has thrust its tail into my engine. If it has caught in the fan-belt we shall need a pair of scissors. Do you happen to carry one?'

'Don't be a fool, woman.' Lady Pinkerton, nevertheless, climbed from her horse. 'And I know you perfectly well. You are the gardener's aunt.'

'And this, I suppose, is the car of the gardener's aunt?' The indignation of Miss Pringle was mounting rapidly, and had produced this sarcasm.

'Impertinence will not be of service to you. I expressly forbade Lurch to have you visit him, or come near the village. Your husband is a shop steward in Swindon, and you are both notorious agitators.' Lady Pinkerton paused, and regarded Miss Pringle fixedly. 'Good God!' she exclaimed. She was evidently very much shocked. 'You even had the insolence to come to church.'

'Your assertions are merely absurd.' Miss Pringle was now very angry. Although a person of sound democratic principles she resented the charge of living in Swindon. 'My business in Long Canings' – she added rashly – 'has been with Captain Bulkington.'

'So much the worse. The man's a scoundrel. And he takes in Borstal boys on parole. He has two of them now.'

'You are again most laughably mistaken. Mr Jenkins and Mr Waterbird are being prepared for entrance to Balliol College – my nephew Timothy's college, as it happens to be. And Mr Waterbird is a Shropshire Waterbird.'

'There is no such family. So stop talking rubbish, my good woman, and raise the bonnet of your wretched little car.'

Although this speech could scarcely be called persuasive, or even pardonable, Miss Pringle acknowledged that it held a kernel of sense. Keeping a wary eye on the hind legs of the horse, she edged round a front mudguard, pressed a spring, and swung up the bonnet. The two gentlewomen surveyed the situation. There could be no doubt about the fanbelt. It was so tangled with horse-hair that the little engine had the appearance of an upholstered object disgorging its inward parts.

The horse made an impatient noise (as it well might), causing Miss Pringle to skip hastily to the side of the road.

'Haven't you even got a pocket-knife?' Lady Pinkerton demanded.

'No – but haven't you? Isn't there usually a knife in one of those things that get stones out of horses' hooves?'

'I am foolishly without anything of the kind.' For a moment Lady Pinkerton was almost reasonable. 'Won't that fan-affair revolve? The tail might then come away from under the belt.'

'I believe if we were to push the car – ' Miss Pringle hesitated. 'I am not quite sure. But I believe that *that*' – she pointed – 'would then go round, so that possibly – '

'Then we'll try. So don't stand gaping, woman.' Lady Pinkerton was recovering tone. 'The horse will have to be led forward while the car is pushed. You shall push. I will lead.'

Miss Pringle, being fair-minded, saw that this was a just and proper proposal. She therefore retreated to the tail of her car. Lady Pinkerton advanced to the head of her aggrieved mount, and urged it forward. Miss Pringle, having given a warning call, pushed. The vehicle's initial inertia almost defeated her, but she gave an extra heave, and it moved. For a moment it was hard work – and then not so hard work. She heard the clop of the horse's hooves from in front. At first they were slow and deliberate. Then they turned surprisingly brisk. There was a shout of rage from Lady Pinkerton; Miss Pringle found herself running with her hands resting only lightly on the boot of the car; she had a sudden and perplexing view of Lady Pinkerton in a ditch. And then car and horse simply vanished from her view. The sagacious quadruped had solved the ladies' dilemma (in the most well-intentioned way) by converting itself into the dynamic component of a horse-drawn conveyance.

Unfortunately there was a hill, and the incidents here described had been enacted on its brow. Miss Pringle had just hauled Lady Pinkerton to her feet – for it would have been inhumane to stand exulting at her overthrow – when a shrill neigh of terror made itself heard in a middle distance. This was followed by a crash, and the crash by an ominous silence.

'He will have broken his back,' Lady Pinkerton said, and it was hard to tell whether her voice held horror or fury in the fuller measure. 'You are no better than a murderess.' For a moment Miss Pringle thought she was going to be attacked, and she noted with apprehension that her adversary had retained possession of a nasty-looking little whip. But fortunately Lady Pinkerton's thoughts were, so to speak, in the right place, and she turned away and ran down the hill. Miss Pringle, who hadn't at all cared for the word hurled at her, but who felt a certain responsibility for the unfortunate state of affairs nevertheless, ran after her.

The car had gone over a low stone wall and lay upside-down in a turnip field. The horse, although its nervous distresses had brought it out in an ugly lather, was standing quietly at the roadside, nosing experimentally at a tussock of grass. It was, however, bleeding rather profusely at the spot where its tail had been.

Lady Pinkerton took the creature – in every sense so injured – by the bridle and began to lead him away without a word. But then she paused, and briefly addressed Miss Pringle.

'You needn't bother about ringing up the police,' she said grimly. 'I shall do so the moment I get home. I shall also put a call through to the Chief Constable himself. He is a fox-hunting man.'

Miss Priscilla Pringle to Miss Barbara Vanderpump

MY DEAR BARBARA,

How very kind of you to send me an advance copy of *The East in Fee*. I have often thought that Venice, chosen as a setting, would educe one of your finest historical novels – and here, I am sure, it is! I shall read it slowly, savouring every nuance of style. And then you shall have what I promise will be my candid opinion!

Meanwhile, I think it may amuse you to receive a short account of my little expedition into Wiltshire. I did get to Long Canings! Incidentally, the mystery of the odd place-name is solved. I got a hint (quite acutely, I feel) from the name of an inn in which I had a peaceful sandwich and a solitary half-pint of ale. It is called the Jolly Chairman. And, of course, one *canes* chairs – either with imported material or with cultivated bamboo. At Long Canings they used to cane high-backed chairs, which required that the stuff should be prepared in five-foot lengths. Hence the name. How interesting these things are!

It is a charming little village, with some very nice people who welcomed me, simply as a fellow Christian, at matins in the small but beautiful church. Arriving early for the service, I was spoken to most delightfully by a dear old man who might have been one of Thomas Hardy's rustics (only he was much more truly devout) and whose duty it was to ring the bell. Sir Ambrose and Lady Pinkerton live in the manor (which is un-usually imposing), and I was particularly attracted by Lady Pinkerton, whose conversation is robust and full of character. I have some reason to believe her to be a notable horsewoman. Sir Ambrose is extremely quiet. Indeed, I can't say that he really said a word to me! But he read the lessons most movingly, in an exquisitely modulated voice. Dr Howard (who is the incumbent of both Long Canings and Gibber Porcorum) is a Howard. There is also a Miss Anketel, a woman of the most pungent presence, to whom I was not introduced.

And now my big surprise. I conversed with our eccentric Captain Bulkington, and rather liked him! We were quite wrong in imagining that there could be something fishy about his interest in detective stories and so on. This in fact revealed itself as a wholly harmless foible, and he is the most gentle of men – as true soldiers so often are. It amused me that he renewed his odd notion that we might collaborate in a novel. And – do you know? – I am almost inclined to indulge him. It might (as you your-self so thoughtfully said) be a kindness, since it is possible that time hangs a little heavily on his hands. (At the moment, indeed, he has only two pupils – but hand-picked, I imagine, since they are both delightful and brilliant young men.) Of course it would come to no more than an occasional letter telling him how he could contrive some imaginary crime or another. I think I shall suggest that he 'has a go' at Sir Ambrose! ! Sir Ambrose is a baronet, it seems, and baronets are always fair game, are they not?

(Of course, my dear Barbara, there is very little in all this nonsense of mine.)

I expect the proofs of *Poison at the Parsonage* quite soon. I do seriously believe it to be the best thing I have done, and it is perhaps a little depres-sing to know that it will sell no better, and no worse, than any of the others. Unassisted literary merit appears to be of little avail in winning any wide public regard. But if something quite extraneous happened – if one of us two was murdered, for example – whatever we had lately published would go like hot cakes! But I certainly don't intend to be murdered, and am sure you don't either.

And now I must (as servants say at the end of their letters) 'close'. I am all agog to get at *The East in Fee*.

> Ever your affectionate friend,
> PRISCILLA PRINGLE

P.S. You may recall my mentioning having been told that the last rector of Long Canings (as an independent living) had been murdered. In fact, it seems that the poor man simply fell down a well and was drowned. Malicious gossip must then have got to work, transforming this simple if sad fatality into an occasion of sinister rumour. It is happily true that the kind of thing with which I entertain my readers (innocently enough, I hope) simply does not happen in *real life*.

> P.P.

Part Three

A Plot Thickens

Chapter Ten

Sir John Appleby glanced up from his road-map.

'Frome?' he said interrogatively. 'And Trowbridge? I don't see why we should be working round by these places at all. They're not my idea of a quick run home.'

'It's only a small detour.' Lady Appleby swung the Rover rapidly round a bend as she produced this soothing reply. 'And, you see, there's the problem of lunch.'

'The problem of lunch?' Long experience, sharpened to intuition, had brought a note of suspicion into Appleby's voice. 'Why should lunch be a problem? These are fairly civilized parts. I'll get out the *Good Food Guide*.'

'Spare yourself the pains. I've fixed us a free meal, as a matter of fact. With Kate Anketel.'

'Kate Anketel?' Appleby's heart sank. 'And who the devil, my dear Judith, is Kate Anketel?'

'You must remember Kate. I was at school with her.'

'You were at a great many schools, if your account of your early years hasn't been, as I sometimes suspect, pure fantasy. They kept on turning you out. It's why you discreetly declare yourself in the reference books as having been privately educated. It was while still privately educating yourself that I stumbled across you. How should I know anything about your Free Lunch Kate?'

'You've met Kate, at least once. At the Parolles in Dorset.'

'I've never heard of the Parolles in Dorset.'

'Kate lives at Hinton House, near a place called Long Canings. We'll make it in half an hour. Kate trains horses.'

'I might have known it. Another Stone in the Rain.' This was Appleby's term, drawn from his favourite poet, for a certain category of his wife's acquaintances. Judith was a sculptor, but these Stones weren't of the sort she might attack with a chisel. They were her inheritance from a childhood lived amid what Appleby considered to be a completely dotty landed gentry. 'I will *not* be led round endless loose-boxes, or whatever they're called, hazarding totally ignorant remarks about race-horses. Race-horses are even stupider than hunters, just as hunters are even stupider than hounds. And the people who muck around with such creatures are even – '

'Don't be so atrabilious. It's only because you're hungry – and thirsty. Kate's father built up – or laid down – the best cellar in this part of England.'

'If your Miss Anketel is a contemporary of ours, most of the stuff will now be dead in its bottles.' Appleby pulled himself up, conscious that this was a disobliging speech. 'However, we'll see.'

'We'll see,' Lady Appleby said, and pushed the Rover up to seventy. Appleby, resigned, sat back and unwound. He deprecated his wife's bouts of regressive behaviour. But he had complete faith in her driving.

Nevertheless – and it was just outside Long Canings – Lady Appleby almost had an accident. Rounding a bend, at only moderate speed, she had to draw up with an abruptness that jolted her husband and herself hard into their seat-belts. The respectable bonnet of the Rover was within inches of the hind-quarters of a respectable horse. The horse's owner, who was dismounted and with one of the creature's forelegs between her knees, looked up with an expression of unrestrained indignation. She was a woman of weatherbeaten but commanding appearance, whom Appleby had no difficulty in identifying as another Stone in the Rain.

'Confound you,' this person said without ceremony. 'Motorists ought to be forbidden to charge irresponsibly around these roads. Happened to me only a few weeks ago.'

'The mare may have gone lame.' Judith Appleby had climbed briskly from the car. 'But that's no reason why you shouldn't have got it on to the verge.'

'I shall complain to the police.'

'You'd do better to complain to your R.D.C.' Judith stirred the surface of the road with a toe. 'They call the stuff loose chippings. Disgusting flint. Disgraceful where there are horses around.'

'You're absolutely right. But our R.D.C. are a pack of red-hot socialists. Waste of time to address them. If you ask me, some of them are at the bottom of the deuced odd things that have been happening round here lately.'

'Deuced odd things?' Appleby asked automatically. Deuced odd things, after all, were his line.

'A great deal of annoyance and impertinence offered to my husband.' As Lady Pinkerton said this, she suddenly struck Judith as being in a state of barely concealed nervous agitation. Conceivably the near-collision had really upset her quite a lot.

'Perhaps,' Judith said politely, 'we could take a message for you. You might care to send for a groom? We're lunching at a place called Hinton House.'

'Thank you, I can manage very well.' The weatherbeaten woman now comprehended both Applebys in her stare. 'Haven't we' – she demanded on a note less social than threatening – '*met* somewhere?'

'Perhaps at the Parolles in Dorset,' Appleby suggested.

'Very possibly.' It was immediately apparent that this foolish joke, designed as intelligible only to Judith and prompted by hunger and impatience alike, had quite misfired. Momentarily, the weatherbeaten woman was almost civil. 'My husband and I have visited there, and so, I believe, has Miss Anketel. You had better drive on to Hinton now, or you will be late for lunch. Be so good as to go past well on the other side of the road.' The weatherbeaten woman was resuming normal form. 'Kate Anketel,' she said, 'has some uncommonly odd friends.'

'Indeed?' Judith had raised her eyebrows in a manner suggesting to her husband the urgent desirability of getting these two ladies out of earshot of each other.

'For example, the woman staying with her now. She had an absurd name. *My* name is Pinkerton.'

'Our name is Appleby.' (Lady Pinkerton – for it was of course she – and Lady Appleby eyed one another without cordiality.) 'And what is the absurd name?'

'Vanderpump. Was ever anything so grotesque?'

'Barbara Vanderpump?'

'How in heaven should I know? Kate introduced the woman to me. But I don't keep useless information in my head.'

'I think it must be Barbara. I was at school with her – and with Kate Anketel too.'

'Indeed? Then you are going to have a reunion, no doubt. I am inclined to think that the Vanderpump woman is presuming upon just such a slight and distant acquaintance with Miss Anketel for some impertinent purpose of her own. It happens.'

'Really?' Judith said. (Appleby, opening the door of the car, endeavoured – but in vain – to motion his wife within.)

'She noses around. She tries to engage our village people in gossip. Some time ago, we had another woman of the same sort – who even had the insolence to come to church. But this woman, Miss Vanderpump, has the appearance of positively trying to *unearth* something.'

'I think I have heard that she writes novels, and perhaps that explains the matter. Historical novels, I believe. So if she comes nosing around – as you express it – after *you*, you must be charitable, and bear with her.' And now Lady Appleby did climb into her car and switch on the engine. 'Since she has, you see, a professional interest in quaint survivals.' She let in the clutch. 'And in outmoded manners,' she added – and steered the Rover carefully past Lady Pinkerton's patient quadruped.

'That was very rude of you,' Appleby said. He appeared to derive a good deal of amusement from the circumstance for the remainder of their drive.

He was not particularly surprised to find that he did, after all, remember Miss Anketel (and that she, indeed, even called up in him a dim recollection of the Dorset Parolles). The lesson of the great Vidocq, who transformed the efficiency of the Paris Sûreté by the simple means of insisting that his detectives should never forget a face, had not been lost upon the Scotland Yard where Appleby had been trained. So of course he recalled Judith's school friend as soon as he set eyes on her. (He even, he imagined, recalled her smell, which was of what he supposed to be called a saddle-room.) It was a surprise, however, to find that he also recognized that other school friend of Judith's, Miss Anketel's house-guest, Barbara Vanderpump.

And Miss Vanderpump certainly recognized him – although it seemed not a circumstance which afforded her particular pleasure.

For a moment, indeed, she had even appeared rather confused. An animated demeanour and much silvery laughter quite failed to obscure this odd fact to Appleby's professional eye.

'But how very delightful!' Miss Vanderpump exclaimed, exuberantly and hazardously waving one of her hostess's over-size sherry glasses in the air. 'Your husband charmed us, Judith. He held us spell-bound, I can truthfully say. And I was *extremely* lucky in being introduced to him. It was at the last *Diner Dupin*.'

'Yes, of course,' Judith said. 'And John came home saying it had been the most marvellous occasion.'

'So it was,' Appleby agreed, with decent conjugal loyalty. 'Only you and I didn't have the chance of much conversation.'

'We must make up for that now!' Miss Vanderpump said – perhaps with more gaiety and emphasis than conviction. 'I've been so looking forward to meeting you again.' She waved her glass anew, to an effect of sending a fine spray of sherry over Appleby's waistcoat.

'The *Diner Dupin*?' Miss Anketel asked briskly. 'Whatever is that?'

'A gathering of people who write detective stories,' Judith said. 'So of course John adored it.'

'Good Lord! A kind of trade union beanfeast?' Miss Anketel appeared much struck by this idea. 'I didn't know, Barbara, that you went over the sticks under those colours.'

'Only as what may be called an honorary member.' Miss Vanderpump produced this rapidly and on her emphatic note. 'But it was all the greatest fun.'

'You were with a friend to whom I was introduced too,' Appleby said.

'Ah – that I don't remember.'

'In what I'd inexpertly call a pink gown. She was going to tell me a story, I think about a railway journey.'

'How very odd!'

'Or rather you yourself were trying to persuade her to embark on it, but she turned the conversation. Perhaps she thought it would take too long. It was to be about a man who discovered she wrote detective stories, and tried to exact tips from her in the general area of criminal enterprise.'

'What sort of man?' Miss Anketel asked.

'A retired army man, who had turned coach or crammer some-where in the country. But that was as far as the story got.'

'It sounds to me,' Miss Anketel said briskly, 'uncommonly like Captain Bulkington.'

'What lovely roses!' Miss Vanderpump exclaimed. 'Do tell me, Kate dear, what they are called.'

'Captain Bulkington,' Miss Anketel reiterated firmly, 'whom you have been so uncommonly curious about, Barbara. It seems to me – I'm bound to say it has already seemed to me – that there's something going on. Out with it, woman. I don't care for mysteries about my neighbours.'

'Oh, dear!' Before this sudden devastating acuteness Miss Vanderpump appeared to flounder badly. 'It's true I am curious about Priscilla and her Captain. Priscilla Pringle, Sir John. You know her tremendously clever books.'

'Priscilla Pringle? I've never heard of her.'

'You *said* you had.'

'Did I, indeed.' Detected in social prevarication upon the occasion of that absurd dinner, Appleby avoided his wife's amused eye. 'Has Miss Pringle encountered this inquiring soldier again?'

'Yes, indeed.' Miss Vanderpump had cast a despairing glance around the room, as if seeking distraction in vain. Now she took a gulp of sherry and plunged. 'Priscilla has written to me about him. And I detect a romance. It is terribly frivolous of me, I know. But the occasion of my curiosity is just that. You see, we writers –'

'Good God!' It would have been hard to tell whether Miss Anketel was indignant or entertained. 'Am I to understand, Barbara, that you have come to stay with me simply for the pur-pose of fishing out such absolute nonsense? It's more than time that we went into lunch.'

This was self-evidently true – and at table the awkward little *contretemps* ought to have been dropped. It was Miss Vander-pump herself who refused to drop it.

'But I must defend myself,' she said. 'Even if it makes me appear absurd.'

'I'm sure it won't do that,' Appleby said blandly. 'And what you have said is most interesting. I hope you'll go on.'

It was with detectable resignation that Judith Appleby picked up her knife and fork. Here – in the heart, surely, of a large rural innocence – her husband had come upon the tip of a mystery. The wretched Miss Vanderpump's chances of not going on were nil.

Chapter Eleven

'I said that I detected a romance,' Miss Vanderpump began. 'And that is quite true. But there is something more. I find something disingenuous in dear Priscilla's account of this – this developing relationship.'

'If Sir John is interested,' Miss Anketel said drily, 'I suppose we must hear you out. But it is an odd sort of report to offer upon the private correspondence of one's friends. Jefferson' – she had turned to her parlourmaid – 'you may put the wine on the table and withdraw.' She paused while these instructions were obeyed. '*Now,*' she said grimly, 'let this scandalous talk proceed.'

'There is nothing scandalous about it.' Miss Vanderpump was disposed to show a flash of spirit. 'I simply suspect something not merely distressing, but possibly dangerous as well. What if this man has turned poor Priscilla's head?'

'That may be your business,' Miss Anketel said, 'but I'm not at all clear that it is ours.'

'Romance is one thing, Miss Anketel.' Appleby spoke with a new briskness. 'But danger is another. No harm in putting our heads together, if you ask me.'

'Then Barbara must certainly continue.' Something in the formidable Miss Anketel's tradition, it has to be supposed, produced this prompt submission to mature male authority. 'Even,' she added, 'if it means no more than knocking our united heads against a post.'

'Of course Priscilla Pringle hasn't anything one could call money, any more than I have.' Miss Vanderpump ventured a deferential glance round the large solidities of Hinton House. 'But at least she is now making a comfortable income. And this Captain Bulkington sounds to be the very type of the unsuccessful man. I've found out a little about his coaching establishment. He might be described as within two or three pupils of mere bankruptcy. And he can't really believe that Priscilla could teach him to make a fresh livelihood out of writing crime fiction.'

'Is that the idea?' Judith asked. 'It hasn't been explained to us.'

'That, and some nonsense about collaboration. Priscilla seems to have fallen for the nonsense, which she could scarcely have done if she were in her right mind. And she has written about Captain Bulkington, and Captain Bulkington's pupils, and Captain Bulkington's neighbours (including yourself, Kate) in the most sugary way. Only infatuation can explain such stuff.'

'Possibly so.' It was plain that being written about in a sugary way didn't please Miss Anketel at all. 'And this is all very regrettable, no doubt. But I don't see how your friend has been made a dupe, or where what you call danger comes in.'

'I don't quite see it myself.' Miss Vanderpump was suddenly helpless. 'But I do *feel* it – very strongly. "Kandahar" – which is the name, Sir John, of Captain Bulkington's house – sounds such a sinister place. Somebody was murdered there – only Priscilla now says it was an accident. And now there is the wicked idea of murdering somebody called Sir Ambrose.'

'Sir Ambrose!' Miss Anketel was startled. 'Sir Ambrose Pinkerton?'

'Yes, indeed – although Priscilla says he is a quiet man with a pleasant voice. It is extremely shocking.'

'Is Sir Ambrose Pinkerton the chief local notability?' Judith asked. 'If so, I believe John and I have encountered his wife.'

'Certainly he is.' Miss Anketel said. 'Rather a tiresome man. But it does seem extravagant to propose to murder him.'

'Only in a book, of course. In this collaborated book.' Miss Vanderpump, by nature so sprightly, again had her helpless look. 'It does seem in very bad taste.'

'May I get this quite clear?' Appleby asked. 'In this proposed joint effort that we are hearing about, a figure more or less identifiable as Sir Ambrose is to be the victim?'

'Yes, indeed.'

'Do you think it is your friend who has thought up this aspect of the thing – or is it Captain Bulkington?'

'Priscilla writes as if it were her idea. But I believe it is Captain Bulkington who has put it in her head.'

'Then what he has put there is something highly injudicious. I'm not sure you don't libel a man by murdering him in cold print.' Appleby paused. 'Miss Vanderpump, you don't suppose that it is a real murder that is in prospect?'

'Oh, dear – what a dreadful idea! But it *is* very strange. You see, if you had heard Priscilla's story about the railway journey – from which all this started – you would get the impression that Captain Bulkington was some sort of maniac who did have some horrid actual crime in mind.'

'I see.' Appleby turned to his hostess. 'Miss Anketel, you must know this man. Have you any reason to think him mad?'

'I wouldn't trust him an inch. But I'd call him cunning rather than mad. Just occasionally, one has heard of a pupil of his passing an examination. I recall one boy who gained entrance to St Edmund Hall, which I understand to be at Oxford.'

'A college of the most respectable antiquity,' Appleby said. 'Its founder was canonized in the mid-thirteenth century.'

'No doubt. But it is my point that the boy probably owed his success to his own exertions. I doubt whether Captain Bulkington knows Greek from Latin.'

'Perhaps he has organizing ability,' Appleby suggested, 'or is a good disciplinarian. Has he a large supporting staff?'

'Nowadays, I believe he has nobody at all.'

'In other words, the coaching establishment is pretty well on the the rocks. In the circumstances, one might suspect Captain Bulkington, no doubt, of having formed some design upon the modestly prosperous Miss Pringle. A matrimonial design – lawful although not perhaps edifying. And all this business of looking around the local gentry for a good person to murder is nothing more than courtship-behaviour of a slightly macabre sort, suggested by Miss Pringle's professional interests. Mating birds – and even reptiles, I believe – go through motions that are quite as odd.'

'That is probably the whole thing,' Judith said. 'John's answers to such problems are invariably correct. It was a saying, as a matter of fact, at Scotland Yard.' Outrageous invention was occasionally one of Judith's amusements. ' "Appleby's Answer," they used to say. It became proverbial. So now we can forget Miss Pringle and her gallant admirer, and talk about something else.'

'An excellent suggestion,' Appleby said blandly. 'Melodrama

just around the corner is always a beguiling possibility. And – seasoned though I am – I've almost yielded to it! But it's nonsense, of course, in point of any sort of sober fact.'

Judith said no more. Her husband, she thought, was a profoundly disingenuous man. He had interested himself in these wretched people, without a doubt.

'We have a backward son,' Appleby said an hour later. They had climbed into their car, and were leaving Hinton House behind them. Not, however, in indecent haste, since Miss Anketel had caused sundry humps and hollows to be constructed across her drive with the aim of restricting mechanically propelled vehicles to a speed agreeable to the susceptibilities of resident dogs and horses. So Appleby was cautiously nosing his way towards freedom. 'He shall be called Arthur,' Appleby added. 'Note the name please: Arthur Appleby.'

'John, don't be ridiculous.' Judith had no illusions as to what was in her husband's mind. 'There's a great deal to be done in the garden. The Bundlethorpes are coming to dinner tomorrow. We can't possibly waste time on these absurd people.'

'But the Bundlethorpes are absurd too – at least I've always felt so.'

'They have some sort of claim to polite attention, which is more than can be said of Captain What's-his-name.'

'Bulkington. And I don't think it will really take up much time. Mysteries don't often take long to clear up.'

'You'll meet the insoluble one yet.'

'No Appleby's Answer?'

'None.' Judith, who had been restoring a handkerchief to her handbag, closed the receptacle with an expressive snap. She rather regretted having made that foolish crack. 'Besides, there isn't a mystery. It's some mere fatuity.'

'Hitherto, Arthur has been privately educated. He is a promising but delicate boy. It is our ambition that he should go to Oxford. New College has crossed our minds. But on the whole we should prefer Christ Church. Arthur's great-great-grandfather, you will remember, was a Canon of Christ Church.'

'And what is Arthur to read when he gets there? Theology?'

'I think not. The boy's own taste is for Military History.'

'You can't read Military History at Oxford – or only along with a lot of other kinds of History.'

'It will be interesting to see if the Captain can put us right in the matter. Ah!' – Appleby had glanced at a sign-post – 'Long Canings: 1 mile.' He slowed the car, and brought it to a halt at the side of the road. 'Judith, would you describe yourself as having your bearings in this affair?'

'Of course not. There are no bearings to have.'

'I admit they're not numerous, but they do exist.' Appleby appeared to have turned serious. 'Let us start from the beginning – *my* beginning, that is. I go to that dinner of all those detective-story people, and two women are introduced to me. We now know them as Miss Pringle and Miss Vanderpump. Miss Vanderpump is very keen that Miss Pringle should tell me about an amusing incident during a railway journey. Somebody whose name now turns out to be Captain Bulkington spotted her identity – Miss Pringle's that is – and tried to pump her on hopeful techniques of murder. That's all I gathered from the two ladies at the time – for the reason that Miss Pringle didn't want to play. She choked off her friend Miss Vanderpump, and talked about something else for the remaining minute or so that I was with them. Now, that's odd.'

'I don't see that it's odd, at all. Miss Pringle may simply have felt that the story, if expanded, would exhibit her in rather a foolish light.'

'It's conceivable. But, somehow, that wasn't the feel of it. Consider this for a start: that the two ladies were led up to me twittering.'

'Are you telling me, John, that it was the most exciting moment of their virginal lives?'

'On that, of course, I can have no information. But pitch it just a little lower. I was the evening's guest of honour, and known to have held a job which probably features in Miss Pringle's stories as positively an august one. In the circumstances, it would have been Miss Pringle's impulse – if I'm not quite astray about her character – to exhibit herself in an interesting light. And here, to hand, was this business of Captain Bulkington and the railway journey.' Appleby glanced inquiringly at his wife. 'Now, why did she shut up about it?'

'Because she'd seen in the incident the basis of a plot for her next

87

novel. And it would be her habit to keep very mum about anything of that kind.'

'It's a possibility, of course.' Appleby was a little dashed by this rapid common sense. 'But let me go on. At the same dinner, by sheer coincidence, I hear of a rather similar incident – and this time I hear it from a very capable woman indeed. This time, Bulkington – or call him just the Bulkington figure – is interested not in homicide but in blackmail. He is doing a little research, in fact, into hopeful ways of getting blackmail going. What would you say this total picture suggests?'

'An eccentric: probably harmless, but just possibly dangerous.'

'Top marks. The next thing we discover is that this fugitive encounter in a railway compartment has, in fact, blossomed into a relationship. Miss Pringle has come nosing around these parts, has acquainted herself further with the mysterious crammer, has apparently met his pupils, and has even cultivated some of his neighbours. Now, what's all that about?'

'Same thing. Collecting copy for some piece of nonsense she proposes to write.'

'Well, writing something certainly comes into the picture – but it is to be in the form of a collaboration between our two chance-met railway travellers. Or so Miss Vanderpump believes. Miss Vanderpump, incidentally, is our final puzzle for the moment. She feels that Miss Pringle has been writing to her disingenuously about the relationship. And she has herself actually come down to investigate, staying with your unwitting friend Miss Anketel for the purpose. I find that odd. Miss Vanderpump might well take a more or less prurient interest in some supposed developing romance or liaison between Captain Bulkington and her friend. But surely she wouldn't give time to downright spying if that was all that was in her head? And plainly it isn't. Her head is full of confused nonsense about possible sinister interpretations of the affair. Bulkington is leading Miss Pringle into a trap which is not merely – or perhaps at all – of the matrimonial order.'

'Or it might be the other way round.'

'Top marks again. One gets the feel, indeed, of its having been Miss Pringle who took the initiative in following up the encounter on the train. And finally, there's the bizarre notion of basing the most improbable and implausible collaboration on the imagined murder of a local bigwig, Sir Ambrose Pinkerton. Or not quite finally. For perhaps Sir Ambrose will *really* be murdered. Perhaps Bulkington is an authentic homicidal maniac, perhaps Miss Pringle hasn't (or has) taken his true measure, perhaps some dodge that ought simply to be tipped into a thriller is, so to speak, going to break loose and rampage around, greatly to Sir Ambrose's inconvenience. Something of that sort floats in the good Miss Vanderpump's vision.'

'The good Miss Vanderpump is a fool. And the good Miss Pringle sounds like a fool too.'

'Ah!' Appleby started the car again, and drove on. 'It is, unfortunately, a statistical probability that anybody one meets is a fool. But that's no reason for simply slapping the label around. I'm rather inclined, as a matter of fact, to suspend judgement about both these ladies. . . . Good Lord! That must be "Kandahar". What a brutally ugly house.'

Chapter Twelve

Inquiring parents might have been very much an everyday affair with Captain Bulkington. He greeted the Applebys courteously, yet with the ghost of a suggestion that only the inflexibility of that courtesy (proper in one holding Her Majesty's commission) dissimulated the fact that they were on something of a conveyor belt. Captain Bulkington was not quite certain there was a vacancy at 'Kandahar', and to determine this point consulted a large register on his desk – rather in the manner of a reception clerk in a high-class hotel. This happily produced a favourable result, and he turned back to his visitors with a brisk cordiality – not unbalanced, however, by more than a hint that, of necessity, a pretty stiff inquisition lay before them.

'Mr Appleby, I think you said, sir?'

'Quite right. Anthony Appleby.'

'Thank you.' Captain Bulkington began majestically filling in what appeared to be a very large form. 'May I inquire your profession?'

'I am a member of the Stock Exchange.'

Captain Bulkington greeted this with a restrained but respectful bow. Judith Appleby greeted it with a compression of the lips. Being retired, she thought, was more and more going to John's head. A freakish and irresponsible strain was liable to erupt in him from hiding-places fifty years deep, and the result was something unknown at Scotland Yard. Probably you could be put in gaol for claiming to be a member of the Stock Exchange: it was surely an utterly heinous species of false pretences. No doubt that made it strike John as all the funnier.

'And you have brought up the young man?' Captain Bulkington inquired. 'He is perhaps waiting in your car?'

'No, we haven't brought Ambrose . . . Arthur, that is to say.' Judith produced this. She couldn't, after all, refuse to play. 'Arthur is rather a nervous boy.'

'Yes, yes – to be sure.' Captain Bulkington nodded in a sympathetic and heartening manner. 'It is unfortunate, all the same. I like candidates to have a look round the place before anything definite is arranged. Fact is, ma'am, I'm keen – really deuced keen – on consulting the – um – sensibilities of the young. Moreover, if you had brought Arthur with you, it might have been possible to receive and enrol him at once. Particularly to enrol him, which is the important thing. However, we can perhaps proceed as far as registration. There is a small fee. A merely formal matter.'

'Of course, of course.' Appleby went through the motions of a stockbroker about to produce an outsize cheque-book.

'All in good time, Mr Appleby.' Captain Bulkington had raised a dignified hand. 'Do I understand it to be your wish that Arthur should be prepared for entry to one of the ancient universities?'

'Yes – to Oxford. We have Christ Church in mind – or perhaps New College. The present Warden of New College, as it happens, is Arthur's uncle. And the Senior Tutor is his first cousin, and the Tutor for Admissions is his godfather. I also know the Chaplain, and give him a square meal from time to time.'

'Quite so.' Captain Bulkington recorded all these striking particulars on the form before him. 'I think I can recommend New College strongly. Just at the moment, the moral tone is particularly good there. Better than at Christ Church, I should say – although that is very good too.'

'I'm delighted to hear it,' Appleby said. 'And I am reminded

90

that we are particularly anxious that Arthur's convictions should be considered.'

'His convictions?' There was sudden misgiving in Captain Bulkington's tone. 'If anything like that is in question, I'm afraid there would have to be a certain amount of special provision, and – um – a special fee. It doesn't normally come my way, Mr Appleby. Not that I am prejudiced. I hope I bear a thoroughly open mind. My liberal views are no doubt the occasion of that damned woman at the Hall putting it about that I take Borstal boys from wealthy families on parole. Not a word of truth in it. But if your son –'

'I fear you mistake me. Arthur's religious conviction were in my mind.'

'Odd misunderstanding – eh? Ha-ha!' Without any appearance of being disconcerted, Captain Bulkington made another entry on the form. 'Religious instruction, by all means. Twice a week, or three times. It's an extra, of course. But I can supply it at a very high level, a very high level indeed.'

'And have you a good vicar here?' Judith asked.

'Rector, ma'am, in these parts. Fellow of the name of Howard. Gentleman, I'm glad to say. And knows his drill thoroughly. Make a point of parading my lads before him every Sunday. Smarten up on the devotional side. Capital thing.' As he offered these edifying remarks, Captain Bulkington raised his pen in the air, as if to emphasize their purport by pointing heavenwards. It turned out, however, that he was merely proposing to hand the instrument to Appleby. 'Bottom right-hand corner, my dear sir,' he said casually. 'And it might be as well for you to initial the small print on the back as well.'

'I think we'll look round first.' The business instincts of Mr Anthony Appleby, pillar of the London Stock Exchange, not unnaturally asserted themselves at this juncture. 'See your young men at work, and so forth.'

'Certainly. Excellent thought, in fact.' Captain Bulkington rose with a dignified alacrity and moved towards the door of his sanctum. 'We may suitably begin with the Oxford and Cambridge Scholarship Class – who are the lads who will be delighted to recruit – um – Arthur to their number. Today, unfortunately, they are a somewhat diminished band. Only a couple of them here, I'd say at a guess. The other half-dozen have gone off to Cambridge. They are to be interviewed by um – um – the Provost of King's College, who is a very old friend of mine.'

The guess proved accurate. In a large and otherwise deserted classroom two young men sat sprawled behind small, untidy desks. The eyes of each were closed, presumably as an aid to intellectual concentration. When Captain Bulkington ominously coughed, however, their eyes opened with surprising speed, and at the sight of Judith they shambled to their feet. One of them glowered at the visitors, and the other gaped. Between them they represented, it was to be supposed, what might be called the working capital of 'Kandahar' as a tutorial establishment. They didn't strike Appleby as likely to make the reputation of the place.

'Mr Jenkins and Mr Waterbird,' Captain Bulkington said formally. 'Mr and Mrs Appleby. But no intention of interrupting your work, my dear lads. *Fugit thingummy tempus* – eh, Waterbird?'

'Yes, sir.' Mr Waterbird, although he was a ferocious-looking youth, answered like a lamb – although a lamb, indeed, in a bad temper.

'*Carpe diem*, then Waterbird. An observation of Horace's. You might look up Horace. Note his dates, and so on. Jenkins!'

'Sir?' The jaw of Jenkins, which appeared naturally recessive, receded yet further upon challenge.

'Be so good as to repeat the definite article in Greek.'

'Hoeheetoe.' Jenkins produced these magic syllables at top speed; he might have been, so to speak, catching them by the fore-lock before they faded in a middle distance.

'Very good, Jenkins. There are, of course, further parts – but in practice they were seldom used. Not, that is to say, in Greek of the great classical period. Eh, Mr Appleby? Brings it all back to you, I dare say. What a grind we thought it all – but how rich was the reward! Jenkins, make a note of that. And then go on to *tupto*. I judge you quite ready for *tupto* now.' Captain Bulkington turned apologetically to Judith. 'Learned matters to discuss before a lady, 'pon my soul! Waterbird and Jenkins, carry on.' The Captain paused meaningfully. 'You understand me, Waterbird?'

'Yes, sir.'

'Jenkins, do as Waterbird tells you . . . And, now, let me see.'

Ushering his guests from the room, Captain Bulkington moved slowly down a corridor, rounded a corner, and paused by a window. 'Next, I feel, the Army Class. Yes, you might well find that interesting. First, however, I would have you admire our view. Influences of nature deuced important in forming the character of the young, wouldn't you say? "Earth has not anything to show more fair." I make them learn that by heart. Spoken by the poet Wordsworth, when on the brow of the mighty Helvellyn. Remarkable poet. 1770–1880. Great believer in dates, ma'am. Not for the ladies, of course, but capital discipline for the masculine intellect . . . Ah!'

The party was passing a closed door, and as they did so the proprietor of 'Kandahar' raised an alerting finger. From beyond the door sounded many voices, surprisingly deep in tone, and producing something uncommonly like a Gregorian chant.

'The Modern Side,' Captain Bulkington said brilliantly. 'Elocution, and so forth. Most important. But we won't disturb them, eh?'

'It would be a great shame to do that,' Appleby said.

The Army Class at 'Kandahar' consisted, at the moment, of two youths, viewed somewhat in shadow, and from behind. Their fellows, it seemed, were out on a field day, since Captain Bulkington was a firm believer in the practical aspects of a military training. Similar considerations applied to the scientists, who were engaged in active geological work. As for the pupils of artistic inclination, they were abroad sketching on the downs.

'But we mustn't fatigue Mrs Appleby,' Captain Bulkington presently said with courtly solicitousness. '*Satis* – eh, Mr Appleby?'

'Very true. *Id arbitror adprime in vita esse utile –* '

'What's that?'

'*ut nequid nimis,*' Appleby concluded gravely. And – in a most unpolicemanlike manner – he blithely forgave himself for earning a sudden suspicious glance.

'We must discuss it all with Arthur,' Judith said hastily but firmly, 'and let you know.'

Chapter Thirteen

'Thirty years of chequered connubial experience,' Judith said from the driving-seat of the car, 'and I discover myself to be married to a clown.'

'Very true. But just move round the first bend of the drive, and stop. I think we'll take a stroll in the grounds.'

'I'd have thought that *nequid nimis* applied.' Judith set the car in motion, and carried out her husband's tiresome instructions. 'John, the only excuse you could possibly advance for poking around in the peculiar life of this locality is a lively persuasion that something really sinister is blowing up. And that's surely nonsense. Unless Bulkington is an inspired actor, he's the next thing to a harmless lunatic.'

'Harmless?'

'Harmless so far as any kind of plot or machination is concerned. His deceptions are so childish that nobody could possibly be taken in by them.'

'That is certainly the impression he has – well, offered us. And offered us, at any rate, very much on a plate. But who knows? Certainly not you or I. More facts are required. Let's get out and walk.'

They got out and walked. 'Kandahar' owned a large, rambling, and extremely neglected garden, full of tall untrimmed hedges and hypertrophied shrubs. It appeared long since to have been abandoned by anything higher in the scale of creation than snails and slugs. At almost every step on the overgrown paths, indeed, an invisible snail crunched gruesomely under their feet. Although the house itself made up in height for what it lacked in any other form of imposingness, they were quite invisible from it as they moved around.

'Wouldn't you say,' Appleby asked mildly, 'that the learned and gallant Captain really wants Arthur?'

'The answer to that is your own: it was the impression he offered us.' Judith paused to brush a cobweb from her face. 'What about trying it out?'

94

'Trying it out?'

'Coming back in a day or two, and bringing Arthur with us.'

'My dear Judith, you forget. You have a number of grown-up children, and if you like I'll run over their names. But young Arthur isn't among them. To put the thing brutally, Arthur Appleby doesn't exist.'

'Oh, but we could borrow him! A young man or boy, I mean. Or hire one. From a drama school, perhaps. Then we could see whether our military friend was merely disconcerted.'

'That's very true.' Appleby had to speak as one impressed by his wife's resource. 'The cramming establishment is distinctly in a vestigial state. Perhaps it really is a cover for something else. Perhaps Messrs Waterbird and Jenkins are not genuine pupils at all, but skilled accomplices in organized crime.'

'I did have a sense that they were oddly under Bulkington's thumb. It seemed natural enough in Jenkins's case, because he has the air of a pretty dim youth. But Waterbird struck me as potentially truculent and tough.'

'Don't forget that Bulkington discusses not merely the techniques of murder during railway journeys. He discusses the techniques of blackmail as well.'

'I didn't gather that to be at all certain. It depends on whether, at that dinner, it was about the identical person that you were told two distinct stories.'

'Perfectly true. Call it, however, what is termed in my trade a working hypothesis. Then perhaps Bulkington has developed a quiet pressurising line on his young charges. Involved them in something mum and dad wouldn't care to hear about: that kind of thing.'

'What a squalid notion!'

'Much in life *is* squalid, my dear girl. I've looked into the question rather thoroughly, and I know.'

'Are you looking into *this* thoroughly – or just idling away an afternoon?'

'Ah!' Appleby found this change of front on his wife's part momentarily disconcerting. 'I admit that most of the work is yet to do. And don't forget that, for the time being, the principal character is off-stage.'

'The Pringle woman? You'd better ask her to lunch at your club. She'd be thrilled. Indeed, she'd twitter.'

'It's an idea. Incidentally, have you ever read one of her books?'

'Of course not. But, as soon as we are home, I can get you some from the county library.'

'Do you reckon people make much money out of writing such things?'

'I'd hardly suppose so. A modest competence, perhaps, for so long as one keeps heroically scribbling.'

'Poor souls!' This compassionate ejaculation was offered by Appleby sombrely to the heavens. 'I suppose they are buoyed up by the notion of one day writing a best-seller.'

'We're all buoyed up by something,' Judith said. 'Otherwise, where should we be?'

This mature reflection produced a full minute's perambulation in silence. They paused to survey an abandoned tennis court, abundant in hemlock and thistle. A lean cat made a sudden appearance from out the undergrowth, and now slunk past; the effect in this solitude was much as if a lion had gone surly by.

'We'll move back towards the house,' Appleby said. 'But, this time, round towards the back. I wonder whether Bulkington is really on from bad to lethal terms with the Pinkertons?'

'He spoke disobligingly about Lady Pinkerton.'

'It was rather that he recorded her as speaking disobligingly about him. Something about Borstal boys. Perhaps Waterbird and Jenkins *are* Borstal boys, being academically rehabilitated. Or perhaps Bulkington himself is a Borstal boy. Seriously, though, I'd be interested in knowing about his record.'

'Crooks have records. Commissioned officers have careers.'

'True – but at times mildly odd ones. Hullo! We are no longer alone.'

They had advanced to the edge of an irregular open space, here and there uncertainly paved, which had some appearance of once having been surrounded by stabling or domestic offices. Here, perhaps, was the site of a parson's house a good deal older than the Old Rectory now known as 'Kandahar'. And this suggestion of an ecclesiastical provenance was at the moment reinforced by the presence of an ecclesiastical person. Perched on a low circular stone wall, which at once revealed itself as a well-head, was a clergyman: lean, dark, and in only the earliest middle-age. His ascetic appearance was enhanced through his being habited in a long and close-fitting cassock. He had a book in his hands, but was studying not this but the Applebys.

'The local padre,' Appleby murmured. 'He must be waiting his turn for Waterbird and Jenkins – to provide religious instruction as an extra but at a very high level indeed.'

'Walk on,' Judith said. 'We can't very decently shy away.'

'Not unless we pretend to be alarmed by the goat.'

This was, in fact, a possibility. For a billy-goat had suddenly appeared on the scene – from where, was not apparent – and planted itself more or less directly in their path. It possessed formidable-looking horns, a singularly wicked yellow eye, and every sign of active belligerency.

'A cross-grained brute,' the clergyman called out encouragingly. 'Its temper is notorious. It ought to be tied up. But you may just be all right if you walk boldly past it.'

Not without natural misgiving, the Applebys responded to this challenge. The goat lowered its head and tensed itself. Then, quite inconsequently, it turned and browsed. The clergyman, meanwhile, had risen to greet them. He gave some hint of politely dissimulating amusement.

'Good afternoon,' he said. 'It looks as if I must thank you for taking on some part of my own duties. I happened to notice you driving away from the house of one of my parishioners, Miss Anketel. And now here you are, benevolently weighing in with the pastoral care of another. As the incumbent here, perhaps I may venture to introduce myself. My name is Henry Howard. And what, Lady Appleby, do you make of the worthy Captain and his select academy?'

It took Lady Appleby, thus addressed, a moment to realize that it was precisely the being thus addressed that had surprised her. Whereupon she intimated to the rector of Long Canings that she supposed they must have met on a previous occasion.

'No, indeed I fear not. It is simply that I have an excellent memory for press photographs. Moreover, I have heard a good deal about Sir John from time to time.'

'How do you do?' Appleby said. This was as civil a rejoinder as he could think up.

'Then perhaps you are aware,' Judith asked, 'that my husband is a notorious practical joker?'

'I can't say that I am.' Dr Howard showed no surprise at this odd question. 'But possibly such proclivities don't readily get into the public prints. Is he, by any chance, up to a practical joke now? Has he untethered that abominable goat, for instance? I should be delighted to hear about anything of the kind. And most faithfully promise not to give him away.'

'Then I'll tell you. John has been pretending to Captain Bulkington that we have a backward son called Arthur, whom we think of sending to "Kandahar". And on the strength of that we have been going round the place.'

'I see.' It rather looked as if the rector did see; and it would certainly have been obtuse to rate him as other than extremely shrewd. He turned to Appleby. 'And you wouldn't care, Sir John, to be found out?'

'On the whole, no.' Although conscious of the absurdity of this encounter, Appleby remained serious. 'Just at present, I wouldn't care to have Captain Bulkington upset or disturbed.'

'Or alerted?' Dr Howard didn't wait for a reply to this. 'Well, well!' he said. 'But it is true that curious things happen in these parts from time to time. I come to this precise spot periodically, as it happens, simply to meditate on one of them. But, Lady Appleby, won't you sit down?' He pointed towards the well-head. 'The stone is quite pleasantly warm. Be a little careful, however. The well is quite unguarded, as you see. Which is curious, considering its history.'

'It looks alarmingly deep.' Judith had peered over the edge. 'But that's no reason why one shouldn't perch.'

And at this, Judith perched. So did Dr Howard; he seemed a man not unwilling to display an exact command of informal manners. Appleby, declining to make a third in the row, remained on his feet, glancing from one to the other of them.

'Could you tell us,' Judith asked, 'just what is the curious thing you come here to meditate about?'

'By all means. It is simply the sad and sudden end of my predecessor in this parish. He fell down the well and was drowned.

At least, I suppose he was drowned, poor fellow.' Dr Howard arranged his cassock more comfortably over his knees. 'So it seems proper that I should sometimes come here and reflect on his fate.'

'I suppose it can be called curious,' Appleby said. 'It isn't really easy to fall down a well. Might it be called sinister into the bargain?'

'Assuredly – although not by me. Gossip, I believe, had it all sorts of ways. But there is no shred of evidence that the unfortunate man met with other than simple misadventure. Indeed, "curious" would be too strong a word, but for one small circumstance. My predecessor's name, my dear Sir John. A name with a good Anglican background to it. He was a Dr Pusey.'

'Pusey?' Appleby repeated, rather blankly.

'Yes, indeed. "Ding, dong, dell – Pusey's in the well." Once one has thought of it, it is a jingle not easy to get out of one's head.'

Chapter Fourteen

This macabre joke appeared to interest rather than amuse Sir John Appleby. Indeed, he looked so consideringly at the speaker as plainly to occasion that self-possessed cleric a certain discomfiture.

'I am afraid, Sir John, that you judge me to have spoken too lightly of my predecessor's untoward end. I apologize.'

'Nothing of the kind. I am merely wondering whether you have been quite frank with me.'

'Frank with you?' Howard stiffened. 'One is not on oath, I think, when in casual conversation with a stranger.'

'Certainly not – and I have expressed myself badly. Let me simply say I record an impression of reticence most agreeably dissimulated. I suppose they got the poor chap's body out?'

'Good heavens, yes!' The rector was shocked. 'And he received Christian burial.'

'Is it possible that an earlier age might have denied him that?'

'You are asking me whether I think Pusey committed suicide. I have already said – '

'Yes, I know. Only – you will forgive me – I fancied I detected you, Dr Howard, to be rather deliberately choosing your words. "No shred of evidence", I think you said. And I had just remarked that it isn't easy to fall down a well. Is it quite certain that there is nothing – shall one say, to wonder about?'

'May I ask a question myself before we go on?'

'By all means. My wife probably thinks you are entitled to ask several.'

'Then here goes. Have you come to Long Canings – and achieved your decidedly odd interview with Bulkington – in some professional capacity?'

'Nothing of the kind – although professional curiosity is certainly at work in me. Call it a trick of the old rage.'

'I see.' Dr Howard looked thoughtfully at the Applebys – as he well might do. 'Then let me tell you a little more about Pusey's death. He had the habit of perching here just as your wife and I are perching now. And of reading his book, much as I was doing a few minutes ago. It wouldn't have been in the least dangerous – but for one thing. It appears he went in for giddy spells. It was some progressive trouble, I have been told. Towards the end of his life he even had one or two fainting fits.' Dr Howard looked steadily at Appleby. 'Perhaps that disposes of the matter?'

'Perhaps it does.' For the first time since involving himself in the absurd affairs of Long Canings and Gibber Porcorum, Appleby looked thoroughly sombre. 'I suppose your own knowledge of the circumstances is necessarily at second hand? It was before you had any acquaintance with this part of the world?'

'Oh, decidedly.'

'You wouldn't, for example, know whether Pusey's habit of coming out and sitting on that wall was an old-established one?'

'I have no idea.'

'Nor of how long he had suffered from his giddy spells?'

'Nor of that either.'

There was a moment's silence. Judith Appleby had got up from the well – very understandably, she found herself no longer much caring for it – and had taken a short turn up one of the overgrown paths, but not so far as to remove her out of earshot. Now she strolled back, and asked a question at a tangent.

'He was taking private pupils at the time?'

'Oh, yes. It is still sometimes a resource in my penurious pro-

100

fession, Lady Appleby. But dying out, I'd say. Stupid boys can't easily be coached and crammed into colleges and so forth nowadays.'

'Dr Pusey sounds to have been not too bright himself – to take, I mean, such an idiotic risk.'

'I agree. However, it appears that his establishment enjoyed a modest success. He even employed an assistant.'

'This grotesque Captain Bulkington?'

'Bulkington's eccentricities have perhaps gained upon him in recent years. But Lord knows what he can ever have taught. He strikes me as a most ignorant man.'

'He is something of a chronologist.' Appleby offered this comment idly. He was picking up a stone, which he now tossed into the well. 'Quite deep, wouldn't you say? I wonder what's at the bottom of it. Truth – could it conceivably be?'

'Truth at the bottom of the well?' There was a trace of impatience in Dr Howard's voice. 'A foolish proverb – but then most proverbs are thoroughly foolish. Folk-wisdom is almost always fatuous. One doesn't come at truth – or not at any truth worth finding – by peering down into dark places.'

'Possibly not.' Appleby seemed to give a moment to considering this generalization civilly. 'But what about the proverb advising one to let sleeping dogs lie? Isn't it your own view that there may be some wisdom in that?'

'It depends on the character of the sleeping dog, Sir John. And, perhaps, a little on one's own individual function in society. To me, pastoral theology may have something to say about such matters. I'd see no advantage in kicking any slumbering dog awake if the result were to be an occasion of scandal.'

'Scandal? Yes. I understand you. And by all means let us forget about the well. Captain Bulkington, however, remains interesting to me.'

'As a psychological study?'

'I'd rather say an economic one. We must presume he was rather unsuccessful as a soldier – and without much in the way of private resources. Otherwise, it would be hard to explain his taking the rather lowly job of assistant in a cramming establishment.'

'Perfectly true. Of course, he may have felt he had a talent for it. Even a vocation. Lady Appleby, you would agree?'

Judith, who may have been a little impatient of this colloquy, had so far braved the goat as to go poking around with a stick in search of such residual flora as the dismally abandoned garden might disclose. Under the rector's challenge, however, she returned to the matter in hand.

'Captain Bulkington scarcely struck me as a born teacher. He must have been on his beam-ends, I'd say, to take a job here at "Kandahar". But when Dr Pusey died – and when the two parishes were combined under your charge – he seems to have been able to take over this house, and what goodwill there may have been – and establish himself as proprietor, headmaster, and everything else. Of course the enterprise hasn't the air of having much flourished since. But money must have been required at the start – and how did Bulkington come by it? That's what my husband must mean by saying there's an economic slant to the thing.'

'Quite so. But perhaps not a great deal was required. Bulkington may have managed to borrow money from his bank, or some similar source. I know nothing about it. The selling of this house, when it ceased to be required as a rectory, was a matter of business with which I was not invited to concern myself. Such matters are for archdeacons, and persons of that sort.' Dr Howard's tone failed to suggest that he held those referred to in much regard. 'Nor – perhaps I ought to say – do I know anything about Bulkington's current affairs. My making free with his garden may suggest my being better acquainted with him than I am.'

'So you don't,' Judith asked, 'visit "Kandahar" for the purpose of giving religious instruction to the pupils?'

'As an extra?' Appleby added on an interrogative note.

'Certainly not. Did the fellow say I did?'

'Not quite that. He implied that something of the kind was available – and at a high level.'

'Indeed!' Dr Howard sounded far from pleased. 'Am I to understand that you included in this charade about a non-existent son professions of concern for the due performance of his religious duties?'

'Well, yes.' Appleby was almost abashed. 'But we didn't pursue the question very far.'

'I am glad that your frivolity was at least measured. The two young men – Waterbird and Jenkins – come to church from time to time. Perhaps it would be better to say that they are constrained to come. I see nothing more of them.'

'Would you say that Bulkington has them in a well-disciplined state?'

'It is not the expression I'd use. A cowed and sullen state, perhaps. There is almost something a little odd about it. Great louts like that cannot go in actual physical fear of the man.'

'I should suppose not. By the way, do you think that your predecessor may have been in a cowed and sullen state – when, for example, he sat here reading his book?'

'How I wish that we could continue to talk further about poor Pusey.' Dr Howard had looked at his watch. 'Unfortunately I must make my way back to Gibber. There are one or two things I have to attend to before evensong.' Apparently about to take a conventional leave of the Applebys, the rector suddenly hesitated. 'About that trick of the old rage, Sir John,' he said. 'I won't pretend to think your interest in this place idle and irresponsible. You must feel there's something it's your duty to clear up. So perhaps I ought to tell you that you are not the first person to have come – ' Howard hesitated.

'Nosing around?' Judith suggested.

'Well, yes. There was a woman who writes murder stories. I don't know whether you – '

'Miss Pringle?' Appleby asked.

'Ah, I see you know about her. She turned up one Sunday in these parts. As a matter of fact, she came to matins. It was almost a suspicious circumstance.'

'Lady Pinkerton,' Judith said, 'regards it in the light of an impertinence.'

'I don't think I'd go as far as that.' Rather unexpectedly, the rector had laughed robustly. 'But Miss Pringle turned out to have some acquaintance with Bulkington, and he carried her off to lunch. For some reason, however, she lunched in the local pub instead – and, as a consequence, had an encounter with Waterbird and Jenkins. Later, I had a short conversation with her myself. There was an impression of the disingenuous about her. I felt her to be cherishing some obscure design.'

'Might she have been proposing to haul something – metaphorically speaking – out of this well?' Appleby paused. 'I do apologize for returning to the well. But might that be it?'

'No doubt she has her own slant on crime, Sir John, and it is of a different kind from yours. What she had her eye on may have been what I have called an occasion of scandal.'

'I hope to meet Miss Pringle again soon.' Appleby announced this with a firmness which was possibly for his wife's benefit. 'So perhaps I shall be able to enlighten you. Talking of the Pinkertons, by the way: can you tell me how Bulkington regards them?'

'Unfavourably.' For a moment Dr Howard appeared to ponder the adequacy of this word. 'Or with a senseless malignancy.'

'Dear me! Have you, incidentally, heard anything about these Pinkertons having been subjected recently to any untoward annoyances?'

'Yes.' The rector was surprised. 'Pinkerton was complaining lately of something of the kind. Vandalism, practical jokes: I'm afraid I don't quite know what. I fear I have contracted the habit of not always listening to Sir Ambrose's conversation quite as I ought.'

'Let us hope,' Appleby said gravely, 'that Sir Ambrose is not similarly culpable in regard to your sermons.'

Chapter Fifteen

The rector of Gibber Porcorum cum Long Canings (as the combined cures were doubtless called) received this valedictory pleasantry in good part, and with further civil expressions he and the Applebys took leave of each other. Appleby himself was disposed to linger by the well, and indeed to give it a good deal of attention. Its surrounding masonry, less than knee-high, was in places crumbling. But there was, he found, a cover of sorts, consisting of a wooden collar and some decayed wire mesh. This was simply lying in long grass, and had obviously so lain for a considerable period. Whether inadvertently or not, the gallant Captain Bulkington maintained within his policies a state of affairs extremely hazardous at least to juvenile curiosity. Appleby was less struck by this than by the apparent disregard of the circumstance evinced by Dr Howard. Dr Howard must be singularly lacking in what somebody had called the imagination of disaster. Appleby expended some minutes, and a certain amount of frayed temper, in hoisting the inefficient contraption back into place. It wouldn't, he judged, save the life of an incautious dog. Or of the billy-goat, for that matter, if he took to doing a little goat-like scrambling. The goat, although it had once or twice given the intruders a further nasty look, was continuing to regard its prime task as munching anything munchable.

'And that's all that we can do,' Judith said. She plainly spoke with the largest reference.

'So that the next job is to give dinner to the Bundlethorpes tomorrow evening? I suppose you're right.' Appleby's agreement was reluctant, but he turned and led the way back to the main drive of 'Kandahar'. Suddenly he halted. 'By Jove!' he said. 'There are two more of our friends.'

It was to Messrs Waterbird and Jenkins that this description was being applied. They had appeared some fifty yards ahead, making their way towards the high road in a lounging manner not suggestive of any lively expectations of pleasure when they got there. In fact they were surprisingly like a couple of small boys who had been despatched in an arbitrary manner and on the excuse of wholesome exercise to the performance of an afternoon walk through unadventurous territory.

'Am I right,' Appleby asked, 'in remembering that Gibber runs to a tea-shop of the muffin, crumpet and cream-cake variety?'

'Yes, you are. I noticed it.' Judith looked at her husband in surprise. It was not his elderly habit to indulge in afternoon recruitment of that order.

'Capital. And now I think you ought to take a healthy walk – just of the sort those worthies have been sent off on. But in the opposite direction. And be back in the car in an hour.'

'Thank you very much!' Judith's indignation was extreme. 'Do I understand – '

'I propose having a quiet chat with our young friends. Over a light but sustaining refection.'

'About *tupto* and the birth and death of Wordsworth?'

'About rather more intimate matters. I suspect them of being thoroughly conventional and right-thinking little blackguards. So a confidential and man-to-man note will be in order. This makes you an unsuitable participant, darling. So – '

'Don't imagine I have the slightest wish to be in on your muck-raking. I shall enjoy a walk very much. And if I'm not back in one hour you may expect me back in two.'

'Good. And, come to think of it, I'll take the car now. The quicker I get them fed – '

'How do you know they'll want to be fed?'

'In an establishment like "Kandahar" short commons are the rule. That's self-evident. They'll make no end of pigs of themselves. And then they'll unbutton and talk.'

'How utterly revolting.'

'Cheer up. I promise I'll repeat every word they say.'

'That's extremely kind.' Judith, about to march off, cast around for a Parthian shot. 'See that you keep square with them: crumpet by crumpet and cream-cake by cream-cake. Then at least you won't want much dinner tonight.'

Captain Bulkington's charges made no bones about accepting an invitation to tea. They climbed into the car with alacrity. Jenkins's permanently open mouth even began to dribble, as if the prospect of solid fare had prompted him to anticipatory salivation at once. Waterbird was more restrained. There was something permanently wary about Waterbird. Sitting in the front of the car beside Appleby, he kept glancing at his prospective host suspiciously and askance. He might have been remembering too late the warnings of his mother or his nurse not to accept sweets from strangers.

The tea-shop was thoroughly satisfactory, being of the kind kept by teetering old ladies in the interest of their health, and, although small, otherwise unfrequented on the present occasion. Appleby ordered muffins and crumpets for a start. Then recalling the existence of anchovy toast and toasted tea-cakes, he called for them as well. Already in evidence on the table was a three-tiered contraption loaded with pastries and éclairs. In no time Appleby's appearance was that of a thoroughly injudicious uncle giving an outing to a couple of nephews from a preparatory school.

And for Waterbird and Jenkins, subjected to the influence of this environment, the years fell away. It seemed inconceivable that anything other than the most innocent depravities could issue from their confiding lips. Appleby, however, hoped for the best.

'And what sort of place is "Kandahar"?' he asked cheerily. 'Can you conscientiously recommend it to an inquiring parent?'

'Recommend it!' Curiously enough, it was Jenkins who responded. It seemed miraculous that articulate speech could issue at all through jaws so inordinately agape. 'Why, it's the most – '

'Ralph means that it all depends.' Waterbird said this very loudly, thereby deftly all but drowning the yelp elicited from his comrade upon receiving a savage kick under the table. 'Whether it's Oxford and all that, or the Army, or the Church, or whatever. I don't suppose Captain Bulkington is equally good all round. Ralph, that's right?'

'That's right,' Ralph echoed, and comforted himself by reaching for another half muffin.

'I can see that, of course,' Appleby said judiciously. It looked as if Waterbird intended not to play. Waterbird was not an admirer or adherent of Captain Bulkington's. Savage hostility towards his preceptor simply oozed out of him. But unlike Jenkins he possessed an adequate low cunning, and knew there were things it would be unwise to chatter about – even in return for the most gargantuan tea. But what things? Appleby, practised in situations even as odd as this one, knew that he would have to adopt a change of tactics.

'It doesn't look to me, he said with a sudden briskness, 'as if many parents of prospective pupils turn up on your tutor. But when it *does* happen, I must say you put on a pretty brisk routine. Waterbird and Jenkins doing Greek; rear view of ditto as the rump of the Army Class; ditto again, mucking around with a record-player or tape-recorder and producing the Modern Side in full cry. Smart work – very.' Appleby glanced from one young man to the other. 'Eh, Jenkins?'

'Ask Adrian.' Jenkins contrived to gasp this through too hastily ingested muffin. 'All a bit deep for me.'

'Well, Adrian?' Appleby offered encouragingly.

In this crisis Adrian Waterbird showed considerable presence of mind – as well as a gratuitous viciousness signalized by another brutal kick under the table. He helped himself to an entire toasted tea-cake, thereby indicating that he at least saw no reason to abrupt the feast.

107

'Sir,' he said, ' – are you really what you call an inquiring parent?'

'Of course not. And you have your wits sufficiently about you to spot the fact. I'd have thought you had your wits sufficiently about you simply to clear out. The place is a fraud, isn't it? Why stay? You're not a kid.'

'Just what are you really, please?' With wholly praiseworthy coolness, Adrian Waterbird reached for what proved to be strawberry jam. 'Some sort of detective?'

'That's not at all a bad guess.' Considering the situation, Appleby decided to stretch a point. 'I come' – he added, accurately enough – 'from Scotland Yard.'

'Oh, I say!' Tucking his shins safely away, Ralph Jenkins produced rash speech. 'Did that old woman come from there too?'

'That old woman?'

'The one we met in the pub that Sunday. Bloody inquisitive, she was. Adrian said so afterwards.'

'Shut up, Ralph.' Adrian's vindictive toe had shot out in vain. Then he looked sullenly at Appleby. 'You can't mix us up with whatever the Bulgar gets up to. We're just his pupils, aren't we?'

'Almost his prisoners, I'd say. And what does he want with the two of you, anyway? Just the fees – or something else as well?'

'He wants a bit of cover, I suppose. Kidding he's a coach, when really he's a bloody crook. And he's got us where he wants us. One day I'll damn well have *him* like that. And, my God, he'll howl.' Adrian Waterbird paused, ferociously scowling. He had resumed his full years again. This, however, did not prevent his starting in on the anchovy toast. Appleby found himself attempting imaginatively to create on his own palate the effect of this delicacy on top of teacake and strawberry jam.

'Would you be so good,' Appleby said with measured severity, 'as to tell me just what you mean by saying that Captain Bulkington has got you where he wants you? I assure you that it will be in your own interest to do so. To be unresponsive, on the other hand, may land you in an awkward situation. I say this informally. My inquiries, as a matter of fact, may be described as wholly informal, so far.' Appleby produced this, he noticed, with the emphasis of one who offers a sop to his own conscience. 'Frankly, Mr Waterbird, it is in your urgent interest to come clean.'

'Honest?' It was with a sudden childishness that Mr Waterbird responded with this.

'Honest.'

'Your wife isn't going to join us, is she? It's something that's not really for ladies, this.'

'That's what I said to the old woman,' Ralph Jenkins said. Ralph Jenkins seemed to make a speciality of intermittent rash and random speech. 'I said – '

'Shut your bloody trap, Ralph, and leave this to me. Mrs Appleby isn't coming into tea?'

'Definitely not,' Appleby said. And he added unblushingly: 'My wife has gone to pay a call on friends.'

'I expect we've been more nervous than we need have been.' Adrian Waterbird was at his wariest. 'Of course, we may have been a bit rough with the girl – '

'Being our first,' Ralph Jenkins interpolated surprisingly.

'*Shut up!*' This shameful and unnecessary admission had goaded Adrian to fury. 'She'd simply been put up to it by the Bulgar – you see? Yelling that it had been rape. And then in he came. Frankly, I lost my nerve. And I've never properly recovered it – not enough to walk out on him. My parents, and all that. Even the police. And Ralph would be hopeless if we were really got into a corner.'

'That's right,' Ralph said. 'It's all really not my thing.'

Appleby refrained from asking whether the girl had been in any degree Ralph's thing. That unedifying episode, at least, need not be further inquired into. Something of the technique of Captain Bulkington had sufficiently appeared in it. And what was conceivably of greater interest was Ralph's reiterated reference to the old lady, by whom he undoubtedly meant Miss Pringle.

'About this meeting in a pub,' Appleby said. 'The lady wasn't a detective, however inquisitive she seemed. Her name is Priscilla Pringle, and she's a novelist. Did you simply run into her by chance?'

'Yes, of course. We'd just slipped out for a drink in the Jolly Chairman. And there she was. Adrian, that's right, isn't it?'

'Not exactly.' Adrian Waterbird had hesitated. He had clearly been calculating where his best course lay, and it was for further frankness that he opted now. 'Ralph isn't very clear on these things,' he informed Appleby. 'He gets rather at sea when there's anything he calls deep going on. Actually, we were told off to shadow the woman, and to nobble her if we got the opportunity before she cleared out. Then we were to chat her up.'

'And that's what you managed in the pub?'

'Just that. As you can imagine, Ralph wasn't much good – '

'None at all,' Ralph said.

' – but I managed to get across the required line.'

'I see.' Appleby had unconsciously helped himself to an éclair, and now contemplated it gloomily on his plate. 'You were to do what you could to allay Miss Pringle's suspicions about Captain Bulkington? You were to represent him as no more than a harmless eccentric – that kind of thing?'

'Not that at all.' Suddenly Adrian Waterbird was looking at Appleby with something like Ralph Jenkins's helplessness. It was as if the limits of his intellectual capacities had been reached, and only bewilderment was before him. 'We were to plug the Bulgar – '

'The Bulgar?'

'Not the word we use ourselves,' Ralph interrupted, markedly brightening. 'But near it.'

'Shut up, Ralph. We were to plug him as thoroughly dangerous. As a homicidal maniac, in fact, who had done in the chap he took the place over from, and who now had it in for the local big-wig, Sir Ambrose Pinkerton, in a thoroughly murderous way.'

'Dear me! And did Miss Pringle accept all this?'

'I rather think she did. I had a feeling we were only confirming what she'd been given a glimpse of already.'

'I see. And would you say that Miss Pringle was alarmed?'

'She thought she was being clever.' It was Ralph who said this, and he had momentarily even put down a cream-cake in order to do so. 'That's something that somehow I always do know. When a person is thinking he's bloody clever. The old woman went away feeling she'd out-smarted us. I don't know what about. But she had at least bought us a couple of drinks.'

'Mr Waterbird,' Appleby asked gravely, 'do you concur in your friend's appreciation of the lady's state of feeling?'

'Do I – ?' Mr Waterbird glowered suspiciously at this orotund question. 'Well, yes – that's right enough.'

'And can you tell me just what, in all this, Captain Bulkington was up to – and perhaps still is up to? Just what was the exercise in aid of?'

'Money, I suppose.'

'Money?'

'I don't believe the Bulgar thinks of anything else. He may talk murder, but it's money that's really in his head.' Having produced this succinct opinion, Adrian Waterbird made one of his ritual appeals to his companion. 'Ralph, that's about the size of it, wouldn't you say?'

'Yes, that's it.' Thus offering his accustomed corroboration, Ralph Jenkins seemed about to return to his cream-cake. Before doing so, however, he unexpectedly contributed a thought of his own. 'Of course he might combine business and pleasure, I suppose, from time to time.'

'The possibility ought certainly to be borne in mind.' Appleby glanced at his watch, and asked for his bill. The little tea-party proved, not unnaturally, to have been a most expensive affair. Nor, in requital of the massive carbohydrates, fats, and sugars spread before them had his guests let more than a few crumbs of information fall from the board. Such as they were, however, Appleby was grateful for them. He accordingly took leave of Messrs Waterbird and Jenkins on a restored note of avuncular benevolence. It was only when he had done so that he recalled having rashly announced himself as an emissary of Scotland Yard. Would they hand on this information to their hatred tyrant, and thus explode the myth of Arthur Appleby for ever? Appleby judged it a fairly safe bet that they would not.

Judith was perched on a stile, sucking a straw, and with an air of contentment perhaps attributable to the continued warmth of the early evening sun.

'Were the young men communicative?' she asked.

'Moderately. Jenkins is too witless to be particularly helpful, but Waterbird wasn't entirely useless. Neither of them has a very clear or extensive view of the affair.'

'The affair?'

'There's an affair, all right. And Bulkington, incidentally, really has turned that worthy couple into a pair of helots. He has engineered a hold over them – by contriving they should behave

111

not too prettily to some local trollop. Not edifying, but I have a notion it may rather establish Bulkington's pattern.'

'You mean that he gets people into compromising, or at least humiliating and embarrassing, situations, and then presents a bill?'

'Excellent. You express my thought very well.'

'Thank you. And now we had better be getting on to the next thing.' Judith jumped down from the stile. 'Mustn't be late for it.'

'Your blessed Bundlethorpes? That's tomorrow, not today.'

'Not Bundlethorpes. Pinkertons – at the big house.'

'Pinkertons? What on earth do you mean?'

'I ran into them on my walk. Kate had rung them up –'

'Kate? Who in the world is Kate?'

'Don't be so stupid. Kate Anketel. She'd rung them up about something, and told them who you are. They were all agog. They want your professional opinion about some disturbing goings-on at the manor. So we're going to drinks.'

'Damn their impertinence. They can confer with the local constable. I'm not in the least disposed –'

'My dear John, the Pinkertons are the hitherto unexplored factor in your mystery. Bulkington has a thing about them, hasn't he? So it's essential you should case their joint too. I consider it extremely clever of me to have made the contact.'

'So do I.' Appleby said this with an air of magnanimous frankness. 'All the same, I flatly decline to go and drink with a woman to whom you were so monstrously uncivil on the public highway.'

'She was monstrously uncivil to us.'

'So she was.' Appleby held open the door of the car. 'But that's rather far from mending the matter.'

'You'll find that over the unfortunate episode a ready veil will be drawn. The effortless civility of well-bred persons will prevail.'

'I don't doubt it. All the same –' Appleby broke off, grinning broadly. 'Good on you, my dear,' he said. 'Let's get moving.'

Chapter Sixteen

The Manor House at Long Canings did not suggest itself as based on any very simple rural economy. Sir Ambrose and Lady Pinkerton, together with their predecessors (whether Pinkertons or not) over a good many generations, must alike have been in the enjoyment of other and larger sources of revenue than would be constituted by half a dozen or a dozen farms. Without the house and within there was much mellow opulence on view. Even the portal-warding griffons on either side of the drive had a sleek and well-groomed air, as if they had lately paid a visit to a superior class of poodle-parlour. The lawns were shaved, the shrubs were clipped, the statuary deployed here and there looked at once respectably antique and rigorously tubbed: one could almost imagine the mythological ladies (who were already conveniently disrobed) as under contract to descend from their pedestals at some appointed daily hour for the purpose of performing the most far-reaching ablutions. The butler who answered the door-bell presented (unlike so many butlers) a similarly cleanly look – partly, perhaps, because he was attired not in ignobly ambiguous garments parsimoniously appropriate to either dawn or dusk, but in impeccable if sombre morning dress such as might have graced a funeral or a memorial service in the highest rank of society.

It was disappointing that Sir Ambrose and his wife, thus surrounded by so much cushioned and indeed gilded amenity, were distinguishably lacking in repose. In her brief encounter with Lady Pinkerton earlier that day, indeed, Judith had already remarked some indefinable quality of nervous expectation not to be accounted for by a mere flint in a horse's hoof, and which might have been held a little to excuse the notable lack of urbanity her comportment had then betrayed. She was much disposed to be gracious now – or she was this until, having taken the social measure of her guests, she had concluded that precisely that was not the appropriate social note to strike. But she was jumpy too. Being naturally of a commanding and even imperious habit, she was in fact jumpy while remaining, as it were, jumping as well. She jumped on the butler for misunderstanding something about the drinks: behaviour in the presence of strangers not to be excused (particularly in the lady of a manor) except on the score of mental perturbation of an uncommon sort. She bore every appearance of being willing to jump on Sir Ambrose if she got the chance.

And Sir Ambrose, if circumspect, was agitated too: a condition attested by something curiously discontinuous in his manner. He had a board-room manner, and a parade-ground manner, and a manner of well-bred hesitancy and reserve, and also a sudden between-cronies manner which kept on bobbing up in the middle of any of the others. He was a very red-faced man – so much so that one was, so to speak, altogether more aware of the redness than of the face: and this lent Sir Ambrose a certain air of anonymity. Although he must have been well-accustomed to decorous entertaining, he betrayed a tendency to stand over Appleby with a poised gin bottle, as if convinced that the sooner the fellow was well tanked up, the sooner would he be persuaded to do his stuff. It was clear that he regarded the arrival of this top policeman as providential in the strictest sense. God, having lately taken the monstrous liberty of afflicting Sir Ambrose with mysterious and sinister occasions of annoyance, had now come sufficiently to His senses to take steps to set matters right.

'Elementary, my dear Watson.'

'I beg your pardon?' Appleby, having been distracted by some interpellation of Lady Pinkerton's, had momentarily lost the thread of his entertainer's remarks.

'Just that. "Elementary, my dear Watson." Printed out, and pinned to each of them in turn. No sense in it, that I can see. Who the devil would Watson be?'

'Who would he be? Well, Holmes's Watson, I suppose.'

'Holmes? Nobody of that name round here. Nor Watson, either. I once had a groom of that name, but he was dishonest and I sacked him. Years ago, that was. Only fellow I've ever had to pack off at a week's notice in my life.'

'Except Lurch,' Lady Pinkerton said.

'Ah, yes – Lurch. Only a few months ago. But that was rather your affair, my dear.' Sir Ambrose turned back to Appleby. 'Lurch was one of the gardeners. Quiet man, but my wife discovered he was related to a pack of communist agitators. Uncle a shop steward somewhere. Shocking thing. Fired him, of course, although he seemed decent enough. Wife and kids and so on. But one can't take any risks.'

'Of course not. Would you say that this man Lurch might be bearing you a grudge?'

'Ah!' Sir Ambrose received this as if it were a very deep question. 'Interesting idea, that. Has its possibilities, I'd say. Cecily, what do you think?'

'Most improbable.' Lady Pinkerton spoke decisively. 'Lurch was a most peculiar person. During his last week with us his quietness entirely deserted him. He went about singing or whistling. And he told me, quite cordially, that my husband had done him a favour. He said he felt a new man. I suppose him to have been unhinged.'

'That must certainly have been the explanation.' Appleby declined more gin, and put down his glass. 'So can we go and look at those exhibits?' he asked.

'Certainly, my dear fellow.' Pinkerton's old-crony manner had broken surface. 'I'll be uncommonly glad to have a professional eye look them over. But not Lady Appleby, perhaps? Something a bit macabre about the effect to tell the truth.'

'Nonsense, Ambrose.' Lady Pinkerton, having taken this opportunity to jump on her husband, produced a vigorous nod which more or less jerked Judith to her feet. 'Lady Appleby is obviously a perfectly strong-minded woman. And has seen worse, I dare say, than a posse of scarecrows.'

'Yes, my dear. Only, you know, the clothes – '

'The clothes won't startle our guests in quite the way they startled us. So come along.'

This conversation, and the refreshment accompanying it, had taken place in a drawing-room of impressive dimensions and general richness of effect. The Pinkertons – Appleby reflected as he and Judith were led from the room – were about as philistine and tasteless as could be, and somehow they would have been less unappealing if only they had been vulgar as well. But one mustn't be censorious; their awfulness was probably superficial and harmless; and if somebody had been playing a nasty and unnerving trick on them they deserved a certain measure of support and sympathy.

'Can you think of anybody else,' Appleby asked Pinkerton, 'who might have malicious feelings about you?'

'I'm damned if I can.' Sir Ambrose had paused to open a green baize door – from which it appeared that the party was making its way into the domestic offices of the house. 'Tenants and labourers all very decent folk, really. I'd venture to say we've managed to keep out socialistic ideas very well.'

'I don't know that what we're in contact with can exactly be described as a socialist idea.'

'Nothing else, I'd have thought.' Sir Ambrose was innocently puzzled. 'Disrespect for one's betters, you know. Dead against sound democratic feeling. But I can't say I'm aware of anything of that sort to complain of. Try to play my own part, after all. Fair landlord, and all that. They respect it.'

'What about somebody in a rather different walk of life, Sir Ambrose?' Appleby paused. 'For instance, your neighbour Captain Bulkington.'

'My dear fellow!' Pinkerton, astonished, had come to a dead halt. 'The chap's a bit of a scoundrel, without a doubt. Little better than an imposter as a crammer, and so forth. Still, a gentleman, you know. Wouldn't go in for this sort of thing. More a matter of cottage mentality, to my mind.'

'I doubt whether "Elementary, my dear Watson" comes out of a cottage – or not if it contains the peculiar joke I think it does. But here, I take it, we are?'

'We have used one of the old dairies,' Lady Pinkerton said. 'Because of the convenient stone slabs.'

The effect was, without doubt, startlingly like a mortuary. On the convenient stone slabs three bodies were laid out. Or so it appeared, until a second glance showed the bodies to be manufactured out of sacking, binder-twine, and straw. Each had been provided with a mask of the kind to be bought in toy-shops, and each mask had been painted an apoplectic (or Pinkerton) red. All three wore male garments of a superior although much soiled or crumpled sort. Appleby surveyed this spectacle for some moments in sober silence.

'Yes,' he said presently. 'The idea's there. It's a sequence.' He took a couple of steps forward, and without explaining this gnomic utterance. 'Your clothes, you say?' he asked.

'Yes, they are. A bit of a puzzle, that. Of course I turn things out from time to time – or my wife does – for the church jumble sales, and so forth. No objection at all to seeing some honest fellow going around the place in my old tweeds. Better than he'd get in some cheap shop or other. But, in fact, these things seem to have been burgled or pilfered from my dressing-room. Clothes pile up, rather. Tend to, haven't you noticed, if one stops employing a valet? Idle fellows, though. Not worth their keep. Lady Appleby, I hope this isn't too disagreeable to you?'

'Not in the least.' Judith spoke not entirely candidly. It would be rational to regard the display as merely bizarre and therefore amusing. In fact, she wasn't sure there wasn't something alarmingly sick about it. What it seemed incumbent to display, however, was cool interest. 'I take it,' she asked, pointing, 'that the far one was the first?'

'That's right.' Sir Ambrose nodded nervously. 'There suddenly it was – dangling.'

'In air,' Appleby said.

'Exactly so. Hanging from the cedar on the lawn – where I came on it myself. With its neck broken' – Sir Ambrose abruptly produced a handkerchief and mopped his brow confusedly – 'or at least looking like that. And looking like *me*. Appleby, I admit to you that it gave me a turn.'

'Most natural,' Appleby said.

'And there's the confounded notice, still pinned on its chest. "Elementary, my dear Watson." By Jove – I forgot! Just have a look at the other side.'

Appleby did as he was urged – advancing upon the spurious hanged man and turning the paper over. It showed four pencil strokes, one of which had been crossed through.

'Three little nigger boys,' Appleby said. 'Or is that to put a wrong complexion on the matter? We move on.'

They moved on – as far as was necessary for making an adequate inspection of the second red-faced dummy. This one had been extracted from a shallow ornamental water in a corner of the park, and a good deal of dried mud and duckweed still adhered to the antique knickerbocker suit in which it had been encased. There was again a kind of label: this time a scrap of cardboard on which Sherlock Holmes's celebrated remark had been inscribed in indelible ink. On the back were two crosses and two straight lines. Appleby looked as if he was about to say 'Two little nigger boys.' All he produced, however, was the single word 'Water', before moving on.

And for the third dummy the code word, as it were, was decidedly 'Earth'. It had been lightly buried in Lady Pinkerton's favourite rose-bed, from which it had been dug up by the successor to the subversive Lurch.

'Well, well,' Appleby said when he had examined it. 'It is at least fairly clear that the four elements are involved.'

'The four elements?' Sir Ambrose repeated the words with deep suspicion. 'What's that – one of those pop groups you read about?'

'Not exactly that – although it's possible that a species of what may be called popular entertainment is in the picture. *The Case of the Four Elements*, perhaps. For there *are* four, you know. Earth, Air, Fire, and Water. It would thus appear that, at the moment, the series is incomplete. Death by fire is missing.'

The silence following upon this pronouncement prolonged itself. Appleby appeared to have no more to say, nor any wish to extend his inspection of the grubby exhibits on view. Judith, who had now decided the joke to be quite as disgusting as she had first felt it to be, made a firm move towards the door. Whereupon the Pinkertons, whom renewed contemplation of the red-faced intruders appeared to have rendered a little dazed, ushered their visitors out. Nobody spoke until they were back in the drawing-room. There Sir Ambrose, having got his hand firmly round the gin bottle, presently found himself capable of more or less articulate speech.

'Did you say "incomplete"?' he asked. 'Damned thing likely to go on?'

'I'd suppose so.' Appleby signified lack of interest in the gin.

'Another of those things going to turn up, and be found in a bonfire?'

'Well, no. This is a very literary affair. You get the technique in ballads and fairy-stories.'

'Fairy-stories?' As he echoed this, Sir Ambrose glanced covertly at his wife. He was obviously soliciting her opinion as to whether Appleby might be mad. 'Don't follow you, at all.'

'Historians of that sort of thing,' Appleby pursued pedantically, 'sometimes call it the technique of incremental repetition. You simultaneously build up and mislead expectation. It's done by chronicling a series of events in which the dominant feature of each is a constant. Always big A, as it were, plus small b, c, or d. So one expects that what will next come along will be A plus e. Only it doesn't. In the final term of the series A has become quite a little a. And there's a great big X, Y, or Z.'

The deep learning evinced in these algebraical remarks evidently convinced Sir Ambrose that his suspicion as to his guest's sanity had been an unworthy one. If he now gaped at Appleby, it was in a wondering and respectful fashion.

'You don't say so!' he said. 'Can't say I've ever come across anything of the kind. But then I don't read fairy-stories – or the other things you mentioned, either. Interesting, however. Deserves thinking about.'

'It deserves nothing of the kind.' Lady Pinkerton, who had been somewhat in abeyance, came well into the foreground with this. 'What it deserves is much firmer action than we have taken so far. What you call X, Y, or Z' – she had turned to Appleby – 'may be attempted murder, it seems to me.'

'Very well,' Appleby said. 'And arson as well.'

'My husband dislikes anything in the nature of a scandal. He is of a retiring disposition. But when impertinence turns out to be criminal lunacy it is time to make a stand.'

'Incontestably so, Lady Pinkerton. I suppose the local police know about this?'

'Certainly they do. A very respectable man was sent out to us. He described himself as a Detective-Inspector. I am bound to say, however, that he did more inspecting than detecting. My husband instructed him that these incidents were to be treated as strictly confidential. In particular, they were not to be divulged to the press. My husband is a magistrate – as I have no doubt, Sir John, you are yourself.' Lady Pinkerton paused, seemingly in the expectation of receiving some grateful acknowledgement of this handsome recognition of Appleby's probable status in the community. 'His wishes in the matter have, of course, been respected.'

'Of course. But this means, I suppose, that no very extensive inquiries would be practicable. By the way, when did the trouble start?'

'Three months ago.' Sir Ambrose commanded this answer with surprising promptitude. 'Odd thing is, the fellow's madness goes by the clock – or the calendar. Noticed it on the second occasion, and it remained true of the third. First of the month, every time!'

'But it's the first of the month today!' Judith exclaimed.

'So it is, Lady Appleby.' Sir Ambrose did his best to lend this admission the casual air proper in an English gentleman when contemplating crisis. 'Uncommonly good thing that your husband has turned up to look into the matter.'

'I'm sure John will do his best. It just occurs to me to wonder whether you ought to have the fire brigade as well.'

'Good Lord! You can't really suppose – '

In mid-utterance, Sir Ambrose Pinkerton broke off. The muted sound of a telephone-bell had made itself heard at some middling remove in the mansion. It fell silent, and a couple of minutes later the butler glided sombrely into the drawing-room.

'The telephone, sir,' he murmured in a confidential voice of great carrying power. 'Detective-Inspector Graves of the County Constabulary wishes to speak to you. I explained that you were entertaining. But he says that it is an urgent matter. He says that it is very urgent, indeed.'

Part Four

The Denouement Will Not Take Place

Chapter Seventeen

Miss Priscilla Pringle had followed closely, if at a discreet remove, the course of events which she had so masterfully set in train. She had done more. For several months now she had tirelessly woven a complex web of which the denouement (if webs can be thought of as having denouements) was at last imminent!

Circumspection, she never ceased to tell herself, was the prime desideratum. There would be those who would declare her moral position to have been equivocal, and even in her own mind there was no doubt that it was delicate. The grand effect of her endeavours, it was true, was simply to be the unmasking of villainy – an achievement which must be held laudable in all right-thinking minds. Moreover, in each of the two phases of the affair she was surely bound to emerge in a sympathetic light. In the first, she was nothing other than a generous woman, shamefully abused as a consequence of having obeyed an impulse of the most benevolent, indeed charitable, order. In the second, she owned a penetrating intelligence, together with the power of taking rapid and courageous measures in a crisis. It would, no doubt, be an inevitable consequence of the whole sensational affair that her name, at present so modestly celebrated, would spring instantly into nationwide celebrity. The film rights of *Poison at the Parsonage* would be sold for many thousands of pounds within a week. The paperback rights (not yet negotiated) would pay for far more than Miss Pringle's customary inexpensive holiday on the Italian Riviera. The novel might even be translated into Japanese. There wouldn't, of course, be much money in that. But one of Barbara Vanderpump's historical romances had been thus translated; and the resulting book had been so delicately refined a physical object that Miss Pringle (a woman of exquisite aesthetic feeling) was consumed with jealousy.

And the next book would automatically be almost as profitable.

In certain carping quarters, therefore, it would be murmured that the whole sensational and scandalous business had resulted in Priscilla Pringle's doing pretty well for herself. That was why she had to be careful.

But this had not been all. It had been some time before she was completely assured of the seriousness of Captain Bulkington's intentions. Captain Bulkington's letters were hard to interpret – since he, in his rather crazy way, went in for being careful too. What if he simply got bored? What if his robustly malign attitude towards the Pinkertons (of which there seemed to be no rational explanation whatever) simply dissipated itself in fantasy, and he turned to amuse himself with other things? And there was a hazard antithetical to this. Far from cooling off, he might hot up, and simply jump the gun. For weeks Miss Pringle never opened her morning paper without being apprehensive of reading about the sudden and mysterious death of a respectable land-owner in Wiltshire. For this wouldn't do at all. She had been obliged to admit (although a shade reluctantly) that it must be only an attempted murder, and not an achieved murder, that was to take place in terms of the seemingly innocent diversion whereby she had consented to provide Captain Bulkington with the basis for an amateur thriller. If Sir Ambrose was *really* killed (she saw with her accustomed intellectual clarity), the sensation, although even greater than it would otherwise be, would not be likely to redound to her credit. No: eleventh hour realization and last minute intervention gave the formula to which she must work.

In the series of letters to the Captain in which she had sketched the plot of *The Three Warnings* (or was it *Fretful Elements*, a phrase she had found in *King Lear*?) she had been extremely careful to write precisely as she had promised Captain Bulkington to do; strictly without a hint of anything other than a literary *bagatelle* as being afoot. And he had replied in the same manner. But three times on the telephone he had spoken to different effect, and been most reassuringly maniacal. Sir Ambrose had really and truly received his three warnings – as of death by earth, air, and water – on the first day of three successive months. Ahead of him now was the real thing. Bang on the due date, and through the instrumentality of certain ingenious measures which the professional skill of Miss Pringle had been able to suggest, he and his pretentious mansion (and, if possible, wife as well) would go up in flames. Captain Bulkington's chuckle just before putting down the receiver upon the occasion of his transmitting this news attained to a pitch of the higher insanity such as momentarily chilled even Miss Pringle's blood.

But that which freezes the blood may be said, in a similar figure of speech, to produce an icy calm. Miss Pringle's was an icy calm. She let the very day come. She let its hour of luncheon pass. And then (having first assured herself that her car was in good running order) she picked up her telephone, dialled 999, and unburdened herself of the staggering realization that had come to her.

Despite thus playing it so cool, however, Miss Pringle was unable to prevent herself from arriving in the vicinity of Long Canings considerably in advance of the time appointed for her rendezvous with the forces of the law. She recalled her collision with Lady Pinkerton's horse and her flat tyre outside the rectory at Gibber Porcorum. It seemed a district in which automobilism was exposed to peculiar hazard, and she must give herself time in hand as an insurance against anything of the kind now. But all went uneventfully, with the consequence that she had an hour to spare.

Dusk was deepening into darkness, and she wondered whether she should simply draw up in a lay-by and compose her mind in solitude. But this seemed a cheerless plan, and she had to acknowledge to herself that she felt the need a little to tune herself up. Suddenly she remembered the Jolly Chairman. There was something heartening about its mere name. And the hour was a perfectly proper one for a lady to indulge in a small brandy and soda. Deciding on this, Miss Pringle pulled up at the inn.

Seeking on this occasion only refreshment and not the pleasures of conversation with local inhabitants, she opted for the saloon bar. It would quite probably be empty, she thought – and pushed the door boldly and regardlessly open. But not only was there company; there was crisis as well. The small square space – not much larger than a commodious horse-box – contained a lady and two gentlemen. The gentlemen were already known to Miss Pringle as *habitués* of the hostelry, since they were in fact none other than Captain Bulkington's pupils. The lady was Miss

Pringle's old friend (and *consoeur*, as Captain Bulkington would facetiously have said), Barbara Vanderpump.

Had Miss Pringle been capable of feeling anything other than a just indignation, she might have succumbed to alarm and dismay before so unexpected a confrontation. Her first impulse, indeed, was to curse her own folly in thus exposing herself in a place of common resort. But her mission to Long Canings was not going to be a secret, after all; and if there was something sinister in the confabulation upon which she had stumbled, it was as well that she had become apprised of it betimes.

And now – even before acknowledging the existence of her friend and the young men from 'Kandahar' – Miss Pringle achieved a rapid preliminary analysis of the situation. She saw that in all probability it wasn't sinister at all. The presence of Messrs Waterbird and Jenkins required no explaining, since the Jolly Chairman represented their refuge from the horrors of their condition as often as they had the price of a pint of bitter in their pockets. And the presence of Barbara Vanderpump could be explained easily enough. It was only necessary to remember (what Miss Pringle had long been conscious of) the appalling vulgarity and triviality of her friend's mind. Inane curiosity and mere idleness were amply sufficient to account for this silly woman's appearance in Long Canings.

'My dearest Barbara,' Miss Pringle said, 'this is indeed a surprise! And good evening to you, my dear lads.' Having achieved this cheerful and familiar greeting to the gentlemen (who had executed their uncertain, nicely-brought-up shamble to their feet), she turned to the pub-keeper, who was making a brief foray from the public bar. 'A *large* brandy and soda, if you please,' she said briskly, and sat down. 'Mr Jenkins,' she continued, 'you don't look well.'

'Not well?' The familiar bemused gape appeared on Ralph Jenkins's features. 'That's a funny thing – because I don't *feel* well, either.' Ralph sighed hopelessly, as if dimly aware of some unfathomable error in logic, and peered into the depths of his glass.

'Ralph ate too big a tea,' Adrian Waterbird said contemptuously. 'And he has a rotten stomach. No good at all.'

'We were stood it by the man from Scotland Yard,' Ralph

bestirred himself to say in an explanatory tone. 'Very decent of him, really. Although, mind you, I think he was fishing for something. About the Bulgar, probably. Do you know, he'd come to "Kandahar" pretending he had a son he wanted to send there? Dashed queer, I thought that.'

Miss Pringle also judged this intelligence dashed queer. It was the local constabulary that she had alerted to the perilous state of affairs at Long Canings, and even if they had for some reason immediately contacted the metropolitan police there couldn't possibly have been time for a man to come down from Scotland Yard, nose around 'Kandahar', and give those two overgrown little brutes tea.

'He had his wife with him, too,' Ralph amplified. 'And the Bulgar said their name was – '

'Shut up, Ralph. You're talking too much.' Adrian's glass was empty, and he now looked hopefully at Miss Pringle – no doubt recalling former benefits received. Miss Pringle, however, had turned to deal with Miss Vanderpump.

'I hope, Barbara,' she said, 'that you find everything in these parts much as described in my letter. It is gratifying that you should think to check up on it.'

'My dear Priscilla, I fear I have not given that quaint plan of yours a thought. And my meeting with Captain Bulkington's pupils this evening is purely fortuitous. The fact is – although I doubt whether I have ever mentioned it to you – that I have a very old friend, Kate Anketel, who lives not far from here. I had promised her a visit for a long time, and at last I have been able to manage it. Hinton House is quite charming, and dear Kate – we were at school together – moves in the best county society.'

'Very gratifying,' Miss Pringle said. She felt momentarily baffled in the face of this unexpected *aplomb* on Miss Vanderpump's part. 'Then, no doubt, you have met the Pinkertons as well. And Dr Howard – '

'Who is a Howard,' Miss Vanderpump said with oafish irony.

' – and Captain Bulkington himself.'

'I hardly think that *he* qualifies as moving in the best circles here.' Miss Vanderpump spoke with *hauteur*. '*That*, my dear Priscilla, must be said, however much it is known that you have been inclined to form an attachment to him.'

Miss Pringle had no opportunity to reply to this disagreeable raillery, since the colloquy of the two ladies was abruptly interrupted by a sudden and unseemly brawl between the two young men. For some reason probably not unconnected with the amount of beer he had imbibed, the normally submissive Ralph Jenkins had turned truculent and stupidly blustering. He had resented, it seemed, Adrian Waterbird's assertion that he talked too much. But just on what the dispute turned was not at first clear.

'Why shouldn't I tell her?' Ralph demanded. 'We told her some damned queer things in this pub last time, didn't we? And that Scotland Yard man – didn't you tell him about the rotten trick the Bulgar played on us with that slut Sally?'

'What we say and what we don't say, you great moron, you'll bloody well leave to me.' Adrian's voice was coldly furious. He was so angry, indeed, that he appeared unaware that Miss Pringle and Miss Vanderpump were not absorbed in their own affairs. 'Telling that chap we were made to tell a pack of lies is one thing. Blabbing about burglary is quite another.' Adrian dropped to a fierce whisper. 'Pinkerton's a beak. He'd have us inside like a shot if he knew we'd been made to steal his rotten clothes. Bad-school, probably, which is a bloody sight worse than quod. They'd have *you* snivelling and yelping in no time, soppy Jenkins.'

'I've had enough of you!' The voice of Ralph Jenkins had suddenly risen to a panicky squeal. 'I'm going to – '

'You'll have had enough of me by the time I've worked over you tonight,' Mr Waterbird hissed hideously. 'Blubbing for your dear old nanny – that's what you'll be.'

'You beastly great cad, I'll – '

'Out!' As he gave this order, Mr Waterbird sprang to his feet – a good deal more athletically than when putting on his polite Kensingtonian stand-up-for-the-ladies turn – and contrived an expert clutch on one of Mr Jenkins's wrists. Mr Jenkins found himself yanked upright, twisted round, and subjected to a rapidly mounting impetus generated by a skilful bumping action on the part of Mr Waterbird's knee on his behind. But the unseemly spectacle was at least of momentary duration only, since with a surprising approximation to instantaneity the gentlemen had tumbled alike out of the bar and (as it was to prove) Miss Priscilla

Pringle's life. For seconds Mr Jenkins's yelping was audible *diminuendo* as he presumably began an uncomfortable homeward progress to 'Kandahar'. And then silence fell.

It was a silence that sustained itself for a full minute. This must have been due, in part, to the shock the ladies had sustained. Neither was without a sense that the behaviour they had just witnessed was quite grossly atavistic, belonging essentially, as it did, to that preparatory stage of an English gentleman's education which commonly comes to a close in the course of his fourteenth year. But a further element in the silence undoubtedly lay in the fact that neither Miss Pringle nor Miss Vanderpump quite knew where each stood in relation to the other. Miss Vanderpump, detected in fishing around at the bidding, no doubt, of nothing better than the most vacuous inquisitiveness, did not know whether to expect severe censure or mere ridicule. Miss Pringle, the very crisis of whose fate had been broken in upon by this totally un-expected encounter, was obliged to calculate just what kind of menace to her strategy was involved.

It was Miss Pringle who recovered first. It would be impolitic, she saw, to keep mum. To behave, that was to say, as if nothing in particular were happening would bear an implausible appearance when, later on, her conduct necessarily came under a certain degree of scrutiny by the forces of the law. Barbara, in fact, must be taken into her confidence at once.

'My dear friend,' Miss Pringle exclaimed impetuously, 'how truly thankful I am for your totally unexpected presence! For matters are dark, indeed. You will be an invaluable support to me.'

'Dark, indeed?' Miss Vanderpump echoed doubtfully.

'My confidence has been abused. Perhaps it is better to say that it has been betrayed. Oh, Barbara – how right you were!'

'I can't think what you are talking about.' Miss Vanderpump was disagreeably ungratified by her friend's generous exclamation. 'And you have formed some very peculiar notions about the people round here, I am bound to say. I take it that the young ruffians who have just left us *are* the present pupils of Captain Bulkington?'

'Certainly they are.'

' "Brilliant and delightful young men", I seem to recall as your

129

description of them. And "hand-picked", as well. Hand-picked from the gutter, it appears to me.'

'Not at all.' Miss Pringle, although aware that the dreadful youths would presently have to be thrown to the lions, was indisposed to admit a falsification of social fact. 'Adrian Waterbird is a Shropshire Waterbird. And Ralph Jenkins's people are of consequence in the industrial sphere. It is true that they have been constrained to behave badly. But at least their ill-conduct has brought me certainty. You heard what they said about burglary? It is something to which they have been driven by the maniacal Bulkington. But now he is to be unmasked! For I have seen the revolting truth in the nick of time. And now I am acting' – Miss Pringle glanced at her not inelegant wristwatch – 'at the eleventh hour.'

'Priscilla, I perceive you to be raving. You must have suffered a severe nervous breakdown. Permit me to summon a physician.'

'Nothing of the kind, Barbara, although I must allow that the strain of the last few days has been very great. Could it be? I had to ask myself that. Could it possibly be? And I had to answer Yes – and that my oldest friend had penetrated to the truth long ago. The despicable Bulkington has made a tool of me. I had supposed that I was assisting him in a harmless diversion. The provisional title of his book was *The Three Warnings*. It was to make amusing use of the fallacious theories of medieval physics. Earth, air, fire, and water!'

'Earth, air, fire, and water?' Miss Vanderpump repeated bemusedly.

'Yes – but that is by the way. Let me say only that the man Bulkington has achieved *in fact* the three warnings with which I provided him for the purposes of *fiction*. The theft, by those unhappy youths, of poor Sir Ambrose's clothes, is dramatic confirmation of what has been going on. And tonight was to have been the fatal night.' Miss Pringle, who had now drunk her large brandy, sprang to her feet. '*Fire!*' she cried dramatically.

'Fire?' In not unnatural perturbation, Miss Vanderpump had sprung to her feet too – having formed the momentary impression that the Jolly Chairman must be going up in flames.

'Do not be alarmed, Barbara. Do not be *unduly* alarmed. The situation is in hand. The police have been summoned. I am on

my way to a meeting with them now. Bulkington shall rue the day'
– Miss Pringle here allowed herself a modest touch of drama – 'that
he and I met in a first-class railway carriage!'

'Priscilla, what appears to me to be in question is a first-class
vulgar sensation.' Miss Vanderpump paused, as she well might,
in this moment of devastating and (in her) surely unnatural
perspicacity. 'You say you have summoned the police. May I
inquire whether you have summoned the press as well?'

Miss Vanderpump had accompanied this question with what
both she and Miss Pringle were accustomed to describe in their
fictions as a long hard look (or, alternatively, as a significant
glance). Miss Pringle returned it fearlessly. There is, after all, a
tide in the affairs of women which, if taken at the flood, leads on to
fortune. And now Miss Pringle didn't intend to let the boat
depart without her.

'Dear Barbara,' she said urbanely, 'I must excuse myself. My
appointment is an important one, as you can imagine.'

'I can imagine more than *that*,' Miss Vanderpump rejoined
darkly.

Chapter Eighteen

Detective-Inspector Graves, as was appropriate to one of his
cognomen, was a man of sombre habit. That Sir Ambrose Pinkerton, a grandee whose powers Mr Graves was unequipped with the
sophistication very accurately to determine, should for some
months have been tiresomely creating about the discovery of two
or three senseless scarecrows around his estate had in itself been
enough to tinge the sombre with the positively saturnine in Mr
Graves's nervous constitution.

Then there had come, from some seemingly deranged woman
declaring herself resident in the neighbourhood of distant Worcester, the vehement assertion, too urgent to be ignored, that Sir
Ambrose was in immediate need of protection against mysterious
menace alike to his property and his life. And now – Mr Graves
having arrived with several subordinate officers in order to preserve
the Queen's peace at Long Canings Hall – it had transpired that

there was already on the scene, irregularly and therefore the more alarmingly, nothing and nobody less than a retired Chief Commissioner of Metropolitan Police. Mr Graves had nothing against Sir John Appleby, a man famous within his late jurisdiction for impeccable relations alike with his most exalted lieutenants and the humblest constables on the beat. Still less had he anything against Sir John's wife, a woman who struck him at once as of an agreeablv composed and sceptical disposition. The situation, nevertheless, could legitimately be regarded as trying to any honest man soothingly habituated (as Mr Graves was) to the rapid sorting out of petty and crystalline misdemeanours of a sort compassable by the yearning but incompetent rustic criminals of darkest Wilts. It was the first tenet of Detective-Inspector Graves's professional code that before acting one must make sure of one's ground. But in this instance it was distressingly unclear to him how this preliminary step was to be achieved. The sensible thing would be to await a hint from Appleby himself. But Appleby, too, appeared to be waiting. Nothing much could be done, it seemed, until the lady from Worcester arrived. She was expected at any minute now.

'A Miss Pringle, she called herself,' Graves said. He had cautiously consulted a notebook before committing himself thus far. 'Would anything, now, be known about her? She isn't on the list of folk who make irresponsible calls to the police. And a pretty long list it is – as you, sir, know.'

Appleby agreed that this was indeed within his knowledge, but offered no further remark. Sir Ambrose, a hospitable if irascible man, advanced upon Mr Graves with a cobwebby bottle which apparently contained brandy of an unusual and superior sort. This embarrassed Mr Graves, who had been taught as a young man that he must not, when on duty, accept refreshment of this sort. Sir Ambrose, of course, was Sir Ambrose. But then Sir John was Sir John. Sir John resolved this dilemma by himself commending the brandy to Mr Graves in a relaxed and friendly manner. Mr Graves accepted a glass like a young football and applied himself, not ungratefully, to the reassuringly moderate tot it contained.

'A most impertinent woman,' Lady Pinkerton said. 'For a start, we do know *that*.' Lady Pinkerton was not only herself drinking brandy; she was also smoking a cigar. This increased Mr Graves's sense of being a little out of his depth. 'She came into our church,'

Lady Pinkerton said. Lady Pinkerton said this much as if she was saying 'She took off all her clothes and danced on our lawn.' Mr Graves, who was accustomed to regard church-going as meritorious and reassuring, was further baffled. 'And it appears that she writes books,' Lady Pinkerton said.

'Like Jane Austen and George Eliot,' Appleby offered, and gravely shook his head.

'Obscene publications, sir?' Thus seeking some glimmer of light, Mr Graves produced a handkerchief and mopped his brow. 'Or merely literature, like?'

'Detective literature,' Lady Appleby said, with a gravity equal to her husband's. 'Which you might describe as betwixt and between.'

Not unnaturally, this appraisal produced absolute impasse. Silence descended upon Lady Pinkerton's impressive drawing-room. It was terminated by the distant ringing of a bell.

'And – damn it – here she is,' Sir Ambrose said.

But the lady presently ushered in upon the expectant company was Miss Anketel of Hinton House. Miss Anketel was known to Detective-Inspector Graves as being, like his host of the moment, an ornament of the bench. This increased his sense that something portentous was going forward, without at all enlightening him as to just what it was. He consulted his watch, however, and resourcefully recorded in his notebook that the lady had arrived at 11.20 p.m.

'Ambrose,' Miss Anketel demanded sternly and without preliminary greeting, 'what do you mean by surrounding your house with lurking men? Fortunately I have come on foot. A horse might have been seriously alarmed.'

'Not men, my dear Kate,' Sir Ambrose said – placatingly and while reaching for the brandy. 'Constables. Constables and sergeants and so on. Graves's people, I'm sure you know Graves. Fact is, it has been decided the place must be guarded. All those damned unaccountable goings-on. You'll take a drop of this?'

'Well – I think I can add to *them*.' Miss Anketel gave a vigorous nod which served at once to emphasize her claim and accept Sir Ambrose's offer. She then surveyed the room and acknowledged the presence of the Applebys. 'Judith,' she demanded, 'didn't you say you were driving straight home?'

'That was the idea. But it so happens that John has interested himself in Sir Ambrose's perplexities. Have you really got something to add to them?'

'I have the explanation of something.' Miss Anketel sat down and consulted her glass. 'That's why, Cecily, I've made so uncommonly late a call. You ought to know about it at once, I felt. And I'd have brought Henry Howard with me. Only Henry felt he ought not to leave the boy.'

'One of Captain Bulkington's boys?' Appleby asked.

'Quite right!' Miss Anketel was surprised. 'It was like this. After dinner, I left Barbara Vanderpump to her own devices – she said she thought of taking an evening walk – and went over to the rectory. I had promised Henry to check the parish accounts with him. It is something we do together from time to time. But we had scarcely settled to the job when this youth burst into the house without ceremony. He was in a state of abject terror.'

'This,' Appleby said, 'must have been the one called Ralph Jenkins?'

'Yes – that appears to be his name. It was difficult to make sense of his blubbering account of himself. But the other youth had been bullying him, and for some reason he had got in a panic about a very queer escapade in which they both had engaged –'

'Stealing some of Sir Ambrose's clothes?'

'I see I am not bringing you news, after all – or not so far as Jenkins is concerned. But it seems that he had been reading a historical novel – no doubt Bulkington keeps his pupils quiet by obliging them to follow such useless pursuits – and there had been something in it about the right of fugitives to seek sanctuary in a church, and Jenkins had felt that church and a rectory are very much the same thing. It was a little awkward for Henry, being suddenly confronted with such a piece of nonsense. But there was something else that Henry appeared to like even less. It was when Jenkins began talking about Bulkington and the well.'

'The well?' Appleby repeated this on so sharply interrogative a note that Detective-Inspector Graves might have been observed to jump and then hastily commit some thought to his notebook. 'Just what had Ralph Jenkins to say about Bulkington and the well?'

'It was far from clear. But I found myself persuaded that this, rather than the absurd theft of Ambrose's old clothes and the using them to dress up dummies and so forth, was what had really broken the miserable Jenkins's nerve. And then a walloping from his precious friend earlier this evening had been a last straw.'

'I don't know what all this is about,' Sir Ambrose said, 'and for either of the man Bulkington's precious pupils I couldn't care less. But what's this about a well? Graves, do you make any sense of it?'

'I can't say that I do, sir. Except that, before my time in the district, there was some fatality, I believe, connected with a well in the grounds of the Old Rectory – "Kandahar", as it now is.'

'Gad, yes!' Sir Ambrose was enlightened. 'Fellow called Pusey – young Howard's predecessor. Managed to drown himself in the thing. Rum business.'

'Precisely so,' Miss Anketel said. 'Of course, it was before Henry came here, and it is something he has never much cared to discuss. Tonight he appeared almost upset by the drivel this gutless young Jenkins was talking about it.'

'Can you be a little more explicit about that, Miss Anketel?' Appleby asked, 'I think the Inspector may have a very good reason for being interested in it.'

'Thank you, sir – precisely so,' Graves said stoutly. And he licked the point of his pencil.

'It appeared to be something like this,' Miss Anketel said, absently pushing her emptied glass in the direction of her host. 'Some months ago Jenkins and the even more disagreeable Waterbird had an encounter with the scribbling woman – whose name escapes me.'

'Pringle,' Appleby said. 'And we expect her here at any moment. But that is by the way. Please go on.'

'Expect her here? Good God!' Miss Anketel was properly astonished. 'But the gist of the matter was that this encounter with the woman represented an obscure stratagem on Bulkington's part. The young men had instructions to present this Pringle person with alarming facts – or supposed facts – about their tutor. In particular, they were to assure her that he had himself made away with the unfortunate Pusey – I suppose actually by pushing him down the well.'

'Drowned him, in fact?' Sir Ambrose demanded. 'I call that a deuced high-handed thing to do. Always knew the fellow was a scoundrel. Often said so. Cecily will back me up.'

'Jenkins,' Miss Anketel pursued, 'is accustomed to having to regard much that goes on round about him as incomprehensible and therefore not usefully to be worried about. That, I imagine, would frequently be his condition in any environment. But it has been particularly so in Bulkington's broken-down mad-house.'

'You view it as a mad-house?' Appleby asked. 'And Bulkington as mad?'

'At least Jenkins does. But he appears to be less impressed by his tutor's imbecility than by his inebriety. He maintains that Bulkington has been mysteriously keyed up of late, has been drinking heavily, and has been behaving in some very alarming ways when drunk. For one thing, he visits the well.'

'Ah!' Appleby said.

'Ah!' Graves echoed – and appeared to write down this ejaculation in his little book. Then an original thought struck him. 'Returning to the scene of the crime, perhaps? It's said to be a common thing. But then, of course, it's unlikely' – Graves contentedly finished his brandy – 'that there *was* a crime.'

'No crime?' Appleby queried – and inwardly concluded that the Detective-Inspector was no fool.

'Well, sir, not just *that* crime. If you push a man down a well and drown him, you don't oblige a couple of young men to inform a lady of the fact many years later. No sense in that.'

'But the point may lie there,' Judith said. 'There *is* no sense in Captain Bulkington. He's off his head. He imagines he murdered his predecessor, this unfortunate Dr Pusey. He nourishes beautiful fantasies of achieving further drownings. The well has become a kind of wishing well, and that's why he haunts it.'

'In fact, the fellow's a harmless, although damned offensive, crack-pot?' This was offered rather hopefully by Sir Ambrose. 'Put our heads together, and see how we might get him quietly put away. Just a matter of nobbling the right mad-doctors, if you ask me.'

'That Bulkington is insane,' Appleby said, looking round him, 'seems to be almost the majority view. And I think it quite possible myself. But, even if he is mad, is he *ineffectively* mad? It would be rash to suppose so. He may nourish fantasies, as my wife says.

But he has a considerable disposition to action, as well. He took action, which I need not particularize, to get these two young men we have been talking about well under his thumb. He made them steal your clothes, Pinkerton, and probably do the job of planting those dressed up dummies as well. There can be little doubt, more-over, that what the inventive Miss Pringle is proposing to reveal to us is further machinations on the Captain's part. Lethal machinations, if my colleague Inspector Graves has understood it aright.'

'Why do you call this Pringle woman inventive, Sir John?' Miss Anketel asked. 'Do you suppose that she has been making some-thing up?'

'At least that is her profession – which it is possible to suspect she has lately been exercising in an unusual way. But we must wait and see.' Appleby looked comfortably round the company, 'I've never much cared for bizarre hypotheses ... Ah, Pinkerton – your door-bell again.'

Chapter Nineteen

Miss Pringle had not, of course, expected to find herself in the presence of Sir John Appleby – whom nevertheless she recognized at once. Hither and thither dividing the swift mind (like the Homeric hero whose guilefulness she might be said to emulate), she tumbled at once to the fact that he must be that 'man from Scotland Yard' who had so mysteriously entertained Messrs Waterbird and Jenkins to tea. That he had now arrived, equally unaccountably, at Long Canings Hall (principal seat of Sir Ambrose Pinkerton, Bart.) was a circumstance which she saw she was likely to judge either gratifying or alarming according to the amount of nerve she was herself importing into this impressive mansion. The presence of so famous a policeman must surely most notably add to the news-value of the strange and sinister events which were about to transact themselves in and around the place. On the other hand, Appleby – she clear-sightedly acknowledged to herself – might prove to be rather a different cup of tea from even a senior and experienced rural police officer.

137

Not that Appleby was suggesting himself as at all formidable now. He had the air of a man who, having embarked upon some social occasion of the most commonplace kind, and then discovered himself to have stumbled upon the fringes of a small family *contretemps* or the like, politely effaces himself until the insignificant disturbance has been smoothed away. Something of the same appearance, too, was presented by Lady Appleby, a well-groomed woman who had produced a fragment of crochet-work, from her bag, and was applying herself to it in a mild abstraction which somehow contrived to suggest that she had come to stay with the Pinkertons for a month, and that Miss Pringle's incursion – oddly nocturnal though it was – was an episode of an ephemeral and unimportant kind. It was different with Miss Anketel, who had also instantly recalled herself to Miss Pringle's mind (or better, perhaps, to Miss Pringle's nose, since the same unmistakable high-class effluvium, as of horse-embrocation by Chanel, attended Miss Anketel's person in Lady Pinkerton's drawing-room as had done so in Dr Howard's church). Miss Anketel from time to time directed a certain grim attention upon Miss Pringle – rather of the sort (Miss Pringle thought) to which she might be prompted by the sight of some coughing, spavined, or glandered jade. As for the Pinkertons, they combined the verbal expressions of courtesy incumbent upon a host and hostess with the stony stares and the pervasive bemusement to which their upbringing and their intellectual equipment respectively prompted them.

All this added up to the fact that Miss Pringle's sensational communication, although advanced in so unexpectedly numerous a company, seemed effectively to be made to the reassuringly respectful Detective-Inspector Graves alone. And Miss Pringle felt she was not going to be intimidated by a Detective-Inspector. She had, after all, invented such persons by the score.

There was something a little daunting, all the same, in the circumstance that it was entirely without comment, and entirely without perceptible change of facial expression, that Graves wrote it all down in a notebook. Miss Pringle wondered whether, when at length she fell silent, she would be invited to sign the record, or perhaps receive some caution required by what are called the